Meg gazed up at Etienne. "How can you be so sure that I'll be able to pull this off?

"You've jumped in and taken me on as a kind of project—one where you're determined to get the blue ribbon by turning me into the best jam at the county fair. You're so sure, so enthusiastic, so determined. Don't you ever doubt? Or question?"

He reached out one hand and raked his fingertips across her cheek. "I question many things in life," he said solemnly. "More than you'll ever know. I make lots of mistakes, and I hate that. I've done things I regret, and even things I can't live with. I question myself every day about those things, but I don't question truth when it stares me in the face, Meg. We'll succeed because it's clear to me that you are an amazing and striking woman."

"And you know this how?"

He smiled gently and tucked one finger under her chin. "I know this because you did something you hated the thought of doing just to save your friends, and I also know this because I'm a man and I have eyes in my head." And without another word, he leaned over and placed his lips on hers.

Dear Reader,

I think that I've always had a fascination with those "before and after" photos one sees in magazines. Yes, I know that often they're not real, or they're digitally altered, but there's something so…hopeful about a person deciding that they have a problem, setting out to change it and then—with a little magic and hard work—succeeding beyond their wildest dreams in a very dramatic way.

So I met Meg Leighton, the heroine of this book, and I discovered that she had a secret desire to be all the things she'd never been allowed to be in her life—and then I met Etienne Gavard, a man who might actually help her achieve her secret desires…. Well, I just had to write their story. But the funny thing is that along the way I realized a few things.

There's no way to take a picture of the "before and after" stages of a heart that's been broken and then mended, but that transformation is even more meaningful than any physical transformation. If we could take a photo of the results, the "after" photo would dazzle us completely. That which transforms us the most is loving and being loved. If we should be so lucky as to experience love in our lives, then we are very lucky indeed.

So, while Meg wants to be a Cinderella of sorts, and Etienne wants to help her, what I'm finding (and what I think *you'll* find) is that they're in for so much more than a simple makeover….

Best wishes

Myrna Mackenzie

Madaris Family novels...*always* sexy and *always* satisfying!

NEW YORK TIMES BESTSELLING AUTHOR

BRENDA JACKSON

TRUE LOVE

A Madaris Family Novel

Corporate exec Shayla Kirland has landed her dream job with one of Chicago's top new firms, putting her in the perfect position to destroy the company that ruined her mother's career. But she never expected that handsome CEO Nicholas Chenault would spark a passion that challenges her resolve—and makes her surrender to the most irresistible desire!

"[Brenda Jackson's] standard of excellence is evident in every scintillating page."
—*Romantic Times BOOKreviews* on *Fire and Desire*

Available the first week of March 2009 wherever books are sold.

ARABESQUE®

www.kimanipress.com
www.myspace.com/kimanipress

KPBJI1270309

MYRNA MACKENZIE

The Frenchman's Plain-Jane Project

In Her Shoes

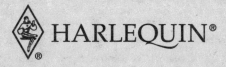

HARLEQUIN®

TORONTO • NEW YORK • LONDON
AMSTERDAM • PARIS • SYDNEY • HAMBURG
STOCKHOLM • ATHENS • TOKYO • MILAN • MADRID
PRAGUE • WARSAW • BUDAPEST • AUCKLAND

ISBN-13: 978-0-373-17613-7

THE FRENCHMAN'S PLAIN-JANE PROJECT

First North American Publication 2009.

Copyright © 2009 by Myrna Topol.

www.eHarlequin.com

Printed in U.S.A.

Myrna Mackenzie never meant to be a writer.

Writing was something that mysteriously famous
people did, and she didn't qualify. Still, fate came
calling in the form of a writing assignment in sixth
grade, so Myrna got out her trusty blue pen and her
lined notebook paper, and penned a murder mystery.
It was titled something suitably gory and…um…
embarrassing (Myrna doesn't remember the title, but
thinks *The Terrible Mystery of the Bloody Glove* would
have been about her style back then). The story was
a mess, and the box containing that story eventually
went missing somewhere between moves (hurray!).
But the experience of writing a story turned out to
be amazing and wonderful and fun and…you get the
picture. She was hooked.

Years later she discovered her true love: writing
romances. An award-winning author of more than
thirty novels, Myrna was born in Campbell, a
small town in the Missouri bootheel. She grew up
just outside Chicago, and she and her husband
now divide their time between two lakes in Chicago
and Wisconsin—both very different and both
very beautiful. In addition to writing she loves
coffee, hiking, cruising the Internet for interesting
Web sites and *attempting* gardening, cooking and
knitting. Readers (and other potential gardeners,
cooks, knitters, writers, etc.) can visit Myrna online
at www.myrnamackenzie.com, or write to her at
P.O. Box 225, La Grange, IL 60525, U.S.A.

CHAPTER ONE

"I HATE to discourage you, but you're not going to be able to convince Meg to come work for you. And I'm afraid... I'm sorry, but I'm not at liberty to tell you why."

That small bit of information was all Etienne Gavard had been able to glean from one of Meg Leighton's former coworkers. It echoed in his head as he drove his sleek black Porsche into a rundown Chicago neighborhood, located the apartment building he was looking for and pulled into a parking spot two doors down. Not an especially promising situation, but Meg Leighton was the expert he needed to help him complete the near impossible task he'd taken on.

"So, this is what it's come to." He muttered the words as he stared at the dingy building where Ms. Leighton apparently lived. He had crossed the Atlantic and had been driven to following questionable women he'd never met to even more questionable neighborhoods. *Do you even know why you're here or what you're doing?* he wondered.

Of course, he did. His calendar said that it was June first. Six weeks from the anniversary of the worst day of his life, the day that would haunt him forever but which especially haunted him in June and July. And for the past two summers he'd handled things badly. He'd closed himself off from the world and tried to drink himself into oblivion to forget the death of his wife and the unborn child she had agreed to bear only because she'd thought he needed and wanted a Gavard heir. Not this year. This year he wouldn't allow himself to sully their memories that way. If he could just get through this one year without losing it…if he could just do one good thing to replace the bad memories…then maybe…

Well, never mind the maybes. The truth was that he'd built an empire saving dying companies and he was good at what he did, maybe even better since the tragedy and what had followed had led him to decide that this job would be his only life and love, his only world from now on. And this year, to keep himself sane, he would attempt the impossible. He'd located a company so far gone that it seemed beyond saving, one where no one cared that it was going under other than the people who worked there. Attempting to breathe life into it would take up all his time. He wouldn't have time to think about the past.

One task accomplished.

Now, he needed the right person to assist him. Usually this was the easy part. There was always someone who knew the details, had some idea what was going on and who knew at least a little about what had made the company a success in the first place.

This time with this in-a-total-tailspin company? Not so simple. Everyone was running around crying that the sky was falling, and the best person to help him, he'd been told by someone with an interest in his success, was no longer with the company. Furthermore, there was a mystery attached to her departure, one that her former coworkers had refused to discuss. But he'd been able to glean this much. The woman, Meg Leighton, was here in this building right in front of him.

Etienne stared at the crumbling brown brick and the unkempt lawn. One would think a person living in such a place would be easy to influence, but no. He'd been told that she would be extremely reluctant and he would have to find another avenue.

"Oh, but I'm a very determined man, Meg Leighton," he muttered to himself as he exited the car. "And I need you, mademoiselle. Very much. I intend to have you." Now that he'd made the commitment to save the company, there was no going back. He hadn't just bought a company. He had taken on the responsibility for people's lives and he absolutely was not going to fail them. That would be unthinkable, the past repeating itself, and it would be totally unbearable to damage another person again.

Besides, most people had tipping points. They could be persuaded once one discovered their weaknesses.

Etienne wondered what Meg Leighton's weaknesses were. Time to find out. He stepped forward and pushed open the door to the building.

"Lightning, there's a man coming to see us," Meg told her cat as she hung up the phone. "I hear that he's French. He's also tall, blue-eyed and very handsome."

Lightning looked incredibly bored. The cat yawned.

"I agree," Meg said to herself. "Who cares about that? Handsome Frenchmen come to our door every day."

The cat simply stared.

"All right, so maybe we *don't* have Frenchmen

ringing our doorbell, or handsome men tapping on the windowpane or…well, let's face it, sweetie, we just don't get too many men around here at all. Even our mailman is a mail-woman," Meg conceded. "But that's not the point."

The point was that Meg's friend, Edie, from the home office of Fieldman's Furnishings, had just called. It appeared that the new owner of the company was going to try to persuade Meg to do something she didn't want to do; come back to the company. But that just wasn't going to happen. Fieldman's had once been the closest thing to a real home that Meg had ever had. Mary Fieldman had hired her when she had only been sixteen and an at risk teenager. She had literally saved Meg from herself, but after Mary's death, the business had also been the site of Meg's biggest and most public and painful humiliation. The once warm feeling Fieldman's had given her had been completely replaced by scalding regret, pain and anger directed at herself. She had allowed herself to forget the ugly lessons she'd learned growing up an outsider at home and in school and all that had followed as a result of her outsider status. The end result of that forgetfulness had been the shame-inducing fiasco at Fieldman's.

Nevertheless, Edie had told her that she should prepare to be wooed by a man who wanted her to return to the scene of the crime.

Meg closed her eyes and counted to ten. "I'll just have to be strong and firm and make him understand that no means no," she whispered out loud. *I could never go back there after what happened*, she thought. The memory of the total humiliation when Alan Fieldman had publicly dumped her, fired her and thrown her out on the street, or that she had not taken it quietly or with any degree of dignity could still make her blush with shame if she allowed herself to think about it. She seldom did. She certainly wasn't going to do so now.

Not for all the blue-eyed men in France, she thought. Downstairs, she heard the outer door to the apartment building open. Immediately, Meg's heart started to race. She had done her best to move on past her life at Fieldman's, to let go of her stunned pain at having lost the business that had been her anchor, and she had come so close to succeeding. The fact that Etienne Gavard's impending visit was bringing back her ugly past…the fear that she might be asked questions about that day at Fieldman's and about her relationship with her boss…the waiting…she had always been so horrible at waiting…

"Darn it," she said, moving to the door and throwing it open just as the man made it to the top of the stairs.

So much for being standoffish. She hadn't even waited for him to knock.

Meg swallowed hard as she came face-to-face with Etienne Gavard. He was, as Edie had noted, very tall. Meg, no Lilliputian herself, was a good half a head shorter than he. With that dark hair, those silvery-blue eyes and that slightly amused smile…

"Mr. Gavard?" she asked, as casually as possible, hoping her voice sounded calm and disinterested.

"Yes, Mademoiselle Leighton. I'm Etienne Gavard. I see you were expecting me a little?" he said, raising one dark eyebrow that Meg was sure made any number of women feel dizzy and disoriented.

A little? She'd practically ripped the door off its hinges. If Meg had been a blushing kind of woman she would have blushed. As it was, her blush was only on the inside. "Edie called me. That is…Edie's a total sweetheart, but she's totally loyal to me. You probably shouldn't tell her anything you don't want her friends to know."

"Ah, loyalty," he said. "I see. I like loyalty." When he said the last word he looked at Meg as if he could see right into her heart where all her most fervent and darn irrepressible emotions lay no matter how hard she tried to repress them. This man was staring at her as if he knew things about her that no one else knew, the places she kept under wraps and hid carefully. Always.

A trickle of panic ran through Meg. No way was she letting some man rip off her carefully applied emotional bandages and make her consider going back to Fieldman's just because he could do that sexy eyebrow thing.

Meg, unable to raise her eyebrow, simply stared. "I'm not like Edie," she said. "Edie is a very special and nice person."

Etienne Gavard's smile grew. The man had dimples. Gorgeous, sexy dimples. Meg almost hated him just for standing here in her hallway spreading all that virility around. She was, as her father used to say, as plain as toast. Slightly plump. With a fading scar on her cheek that had caused her grief in her youth. And worst of all, an outspoken manner and attitude that had gotten her in trouble and kept her there all her life.

"I'm happy that on only ten seconds' acquaintance that you're willing to share that bit of information with me, but…are you trying to tell me that you would be disloyal to Edie?"

Meg blinked. "I would never harm Edie."

He nodded. "Excellent! Because Edie is one of my employees now. I have to have her best interests at heart, so the fact that you would care about her welfare is a very good thing to know. I like loyalty in my employees and…I'm hiring. I'd like to discuss hiring *you*." The man tilted his head. He studied Meg closely.

Meg felt suddenly naked. She most definitely didn't want to feel naked in front of a man like this. "I'm afraid that's not possible. Mr. Gavard, let me be frank. You obviously went to all the trouble of coming from France to buy a company, so you must be an incredibly busy and important man. I'm flattered that you would want to hire me, but I just… I don't want to waste your time."

"You're not." His voice was very deep with that enticing accent. Meg glanced up at him. That was a mistake, since she noticed the breadth of his shoulders and immediately felt a forbidden thrill slip through her body. Men who were that good-looking made her nervous. They were on her "don't touch, don't even notice" list. Especially since that incident with Alan Fieldman. Besides, she didn't want or need to notice anything more about this man. He'd be gone in minutes.

"Mademoiselle Leighton, I understand that this…my methods today are…abrupt and unconventional, but the situation at Fieldman's is complex. I'm not sure how much Edie or any of the others understands about this, but… Is there somewhere we can go to talk?" he asked. "I don't want to alarm you by suggesting your apartment, but surely…"

"I'm never alarmed," Meg said, lying. "And it's not as if you're a stranger. You own Fieldman's. You're Edie's boss. Still, I'm sorry, but there's no point in the two of us continuing this conversation. I don't have any idea why you would want me to come back to Fieldman's, other than the story Edie told me about you needing an expert on the company, but if that's the case, then I'm afraid you're mistaken. I'm not who you need."

"Who is?" he asked, studying her intently. Meg almost felt as if she couldn't tear her gaze away. As if she had no brains or self-control at all, her heart began to pound in a terribly disconcerting way. She ignored it. She'd always had brains, and she was working on the self-control. It was, in fact, the prime goal of her life, to escape her past and become a strong, successful woman. Eliminating her too impetuous, reactive ways was a necessary part of that plan. Self-control was key.

She hesitated.

Etienne raised that dark, expressive eyebrow again, and Meg's breathing hitched in her throat. She wondered just how many strong women he had won over with that seemingly insignificant move. "I'm truly sorry for this intrusion, Mademoiselle Leighton, but the company seems to be in total disarray," he said. "The books are in arrears, production has all but shut down, confusion reigns. Even the most mundane things are out of order. There's not even any soap in the washroom, and no one seems to know where it's kept."

"Third aisle of the stockroom on the fourth shelf from the bottom. Or at least that's where it *was* kept," she said.

He smiled. "See. You know things."

"No," she said, trying not to smile at his blatant attempt to stroke her ego. "I know how things *were* when I was there, but I've been gone for a year. Besides, Mr. Gavard, I hardly think that knowing where the soap is kept is going to help you very much."

"When I wash my hands it will help," he said with that low, sexy voice that made it sound as if he was talking about far less mundane things than where supplies were kept. "But you're right. I'm looking for very much more than soap. I'm looking for someone who's willing to begin an adventure and make a difference in people's lives."

Meg shook her head. "You're obviously way more misinformed than I thought you were, Mr. Gavard, if you think I'm capable of any of those things, and…" She blew out her breath in a slight sigh.

He waited as she chose her words. Or at least she thought he was waiting. "Why don't you want to come back?" he asked suddenly.

She chose the easiest answer. "I have a new job, you know. I've been there for a year, ever since I left Fieldman's."

"Edie said you worked in the office of a local fruit and vegetable market."

"And I fill in at the store sometimes, as well," she admitted. "I like it. Fieldman's is in my past. Gina's Fruits and Vegetables is my present. I like stocking the bins. It's a useful task."

She stared at him defiantly, hoping she sounded convincing and that he would simply go. But he didn't budge. Instead he stared at her with a serious, solemn, contemplative expression. Those long-lashed silver-blue eyes studied her as if analyzing each part of her, and Meg did her best not to squirm. She knew what he was seeing: an overly tall, plump and squarely-built, very plain woman with hips and a mouth that were both too wide and a host of other scars, visible and otherwise. She'd been examined and found wanting all of her life, but Etienne didn't seem to be examining her in quite the same way as she was used to, and in the end, after his perusal, it was her hands that he brought his gaze back to.

She forced herself not to clench them, knowing that the nails were broken from opening cartons and from mishaps with the bins. Meg wasn't a vain person at all, but if she had ever had a body part that she might have been proud of, it was her hands. The rest of her was awkward, but her hands could be graceful. Now, of course, they looked hideous, but Etienne Gavard was studying them so intently that her fingertips started to tingle.

"So, this is your present," he finally said. "I see. You want a useful job. That's understandable. But you don't think it would be…useful to go out on a limb and try to help me save your former colleagues' jobs and keep them from losing all they have?"

Meg froze, her own concerns set aside. "Is that what's going to happen?" She could barely whisper the words.

He held out his hands. "I've seen the work that Fieldman's used to do. I know of Mary Fieldman. She was a powerhouse and a woman with talent and she also had an eye for talent in others. Her company did very good work right up until the day she died."

"I know." Meg couldn't quite keep the pride and affection out of her voice. She missed Mary…every day.

"Edie said that Mary was…attached to you, that you had been there since you were sixteen and you were her favorite employee, that Mary consulted with you on decisions."

Meg shook her head. "That Edie," she said.

"It's not true?"

She shrugged. "Yes, it's true, but Mary didn't really need my input. She always knew exactly what she wanted for Fieldman's. She wanted quality, to sell a product that exuded exquisite class. She wanted the name Fieldman's to mean something extraordinary to potential customers."

"Have you seen what Fieldman's has been selling—or trying to sell—lately?"

She hadn't. "Edie mentioned that there had been a few changes, but no, I haven't personally seen the product. She and I don't discuss Fieldman's, as a rule."

Etienne reached in the pocket of his black suit jacket and pulled out a glossy brochure. He held it out to her.

Meg took it and flipped it open. Both eyebrows raised and she flipped another page. "Is this real? Are those actually wide-eyed urchins on that upholstery? Koala bears? Puppies with pink bows around their necks?"

The pained look on Etienne Gavard's face said it all. "I understand that Alan Fieldman had his own ideas. He wanted to go in a different direction, capture a younger audience."

Yes, well, Alan had always wanted to rebel against his mother. He'd fought hard and used people like Meg to make sure his mother had placed the company in his hands and not his brother's. And he hadn't known very much about young people even when he'd been a young person.

"Help me bring back the company, Meg," Etienne Gavard said.

She looked up into his eyes and they were so blue, so compelling that she almost leaned forward.

"You don't understand," she said, forcing herself to take a step back instead of forward.

"Make me understand."

"I didn't walk away from Fieldman's. I was fired for insubordination. It was a major scene. I made a lot of noise when I went. I fought. I yelled. I didn't go quietly. Everyone was there."

"I see."

No, how could he see? He hadn't been there to

witness how ugly and demeaning it had been. How reminiscent of an earlier period of her life she had tried so hard to fight free of.

"So you see why I wouldn't be a good candidate for the job you're trying to fill."

He slowly shook his head. "You said you fought. I need a fighter, Meg. I want one."

Her throat began to close.

"I don't think you understand what you're saying or what I'm saying. I think I might have even thrown something at Alan."

Was that a smile on the dratted man's face? "Okay, we'll work on that. No throwing things."

"I…"

Suddenly it was all too much. Too soon. The plan she had tried to stick by, to move forward by living quietly and closing off a lot of doors, was going awry. Emotion, a desire for things she had set aside as unrealistic dreams, was trying to push at her. Meg blinked, trying to compose herself.

"Why are you doing this?" she asked suddenly. "I mean…look at you. You're obviously well dressed, cultured, rich if you could afford to come all the way here and buy an entire company. Why would you do that? Why would you come all the way to America and throw your money away on what might well be a losing venture?"

It was a bold and nosy question for a potential employee to ask, but there was too much at stake here. She'd had doors slammed in her face too many times just when she'd seemed to be nearing her goal, and Etienne Gavard's offer had come out of the blue and seemed too good to be true. She needed facts, truth, a

sense that she wasn't going to walk blindly into an incredibly stupid situation the way she had before.

So despite the rudeness and total impropriety of her question, she stood her ground. She watched as a fleeting look of pain darkened Etienne Gavard's eyes before a mask came down and he shook his head. "I came here because… Let's just say that money isn't the issue. At least not for me. Salvaging companies is what I do. It's a challenge, an occupation, and I'm good at it. I usually win."

"But not always."

"No, not always, Meg. And I'll be honest. Even with your help, there's a good chance I'll lose this time."

And Edie and all the others would lose their jobs, the little bit of security they had in their lives. That was so unfair, so totally, entirely wrong and frightening. And…there was another truth that she hadn't dared to face.

If the company was going down because Alan had been running it—

She, like it or not, willingly or not, had been instrumental in Alan ending up as CEO. The thought was like a blow. She wanted to close her eyes, but that would be cowardly. *Fieldman's was failing. Good, innocent people would suffer if it failed.*

Meg wanted to keep that tragedy from happening. If there was any chance at all that she could do something to help…but was that even possible? *Could* she help?

How could she *not* try to help? Edie was her best friend.

"How can you be sure I can make a difference?"

He shook his head. "I can't. There are no guarantees in life. Ever." Again, that fleeting look of pain crossed his face. He looked away and then back.

"But if we do nothing, I can tell you that Fieldman's will most likely go under. We have to try to reverse things," he told her. "People's livelihoods really are at stake. So, what would it take to convince you? What is it that you want?"

By now, Meg knew she had no choice. She had to help if she could, but… She studied Etienne Gavard. He was a successful man, a powerful man, one who never would have ended up in the situation she had ended up in at Fieldman's. He knew things and he oozed confidence, success, knowledge, stability. She had questioned his methods, but in truth, there was something about him that made a person think he was bound to succeed. Etienne Gavard was a man to be reckoned with.

Meg thought about that, about all the things she'd locked away in her soul and decided were undoable. Now here was a task and an opportunity she couldn't turn away from. The truth was that what she really wanted most in life was a home brimming with love and children, the kind she'd never had and probably never would have, but this man couldn't give her that. No one could, and she was grown-up enough to have made peace with that knowledge, so…

"I'd like… What I want is security, a place that's all my own and I want to build a position in the business world that can't easily be taken away from me on someone else's whim. I want to be not just good behind the scenes but also out in the open, a force to be reckoned with, the kind of person that people want to do business with, one they respect. Can you do that for me? Can you teach me to be a success? Tutor me? Teach me what you know and show me the ropes while we do our best to save Fieldman's?"

He didn't even hesitate even though she was pretty sure he wouldn't have expected a request like this. "If that's what you want, then I'll do my best to turn you into a stellar businesswoman."

"What happens when this is over?"

"That would be up to you. If you suited and you wished to stay once the company was on its feet and I returned to France, that would be your choice. And if you only wished to stay as long as necessary to help me get the company back on its feet, I would pay you well and then let you go…wherever you wanted to go. I'd make sure you had a good leadership position, of course, if your training proceeds as both of us hope it will."

Meg let that sink in. This was all proceeding so darn fast. "Do I have to give you my answer now?" Having been given the whole story about Fieldman's, Meg now felt the urge to rush ahead and say yes, but it was that very urge to rush that stopped her. Rushing in had never worked out well for her. A smart woman would at least mull over the situation for a few hours to make sure she had covered all the bases and knew the whole story.

He smiled.

"What?"

"'Do I have to give you my answer now?' is a much better response than the one you were giving me a few minutes ago."

"You're a rather persuasive man." Which might be dangerous under other conditions, but there was no way a man like Etienne Gavard would be thinking of her in any physical or romantic way, so she was safe. Knowing she wouldn't be his type could be rather freeing, she supposed. She wouldn't have to warn herself about thinking of him as anything other than an employer.

"But you haven't answered my question. How much time do I have before you need to know?"

"Let's say tomorrow. The sooner the better."

"Because the company is sinking."

"Yes. Rather quickly."

"Oh, heck." Meg blew out a breath, closed her eyes and did the very thing that had cost her so much in the past. She plunged in. "I'm *not*—I just can't walk away when Edie and the others are at risk if there's even a whisper of a chance that I can help. And…I don't know how in the world anything I do might help save them, but I'll try. I'll do my part."

"So, we have a deal." He held out his hand. His very large, long-fingered masculine hand.

She hesitated, but only for a second. What was the risk, after all? She wouldn't be foolish enough to start having romantic dreams about Etienne Gavard.

Meg placed her hand in his. The jolt she felt was expected. The extreme intensity of it was not. An unanticipated thrill ran down her arm, through her body and all the way to her toes. Every inch of her being felt as if it was humming. Were all French males this potent?

"I'll see you in the morning, Meg," he said. "I'll pick you up at eight."

"I know the way to Fieldman's, Mr. Gavard."

"Etienne. Call me Etienne. We're partners in this venture, Meg. And we'll be working side by side around the clock…on the Fieldman project and on your project as well. I'll pick you up."

He glanced down then, and Meg realized that Lightning had come out of the apartment onto the landing.

"You have a cat?" Etienne asked.

She laughed. "I'm not sure that I have a cat. Lightning

has an attitude. Sometimes it's more like she has a human than the other way around."

"Lightning?" he asked. "She looks a bit lethargic."

Meg shrugged. Lightning usually *was* lethargic, but knowing her cat's moods, that wasn't the term she would have used in this instance. Lightning was slowly, very slowly curling herself around Etienne's leg in what could only be called an affectionate manner. "She doesn't usually like men."

"Ah. Then maybe you've simply been hanging around with a poor class of men."

Meg couldn't help herself then. She laughed.

"Did I say something amusing, Meg?"

"A little." He'd also said something truthful. Besides Alan, Meg had experienced several other catastrophes with the opposite sex; men who flitted away when the next new and better woman came along. So…no more. She'd sworn off men. Fortunately Etienne was her boss. Despite her no men policy, bosses didn't count. They were allowed.

"Someday I'll ask you to explain why you laughed. I'll see you tomorrow," Etienne told her as he left.

When he was gone, the hall felt suddenly empty, bereft of those broad shoulders and all that overwhelmingly male anatomy. The right type of male if her cat was to be believed. Lightning sat on the top stair as if waiting for him to return.

"Forget it," Meg told her cat. "He's not for us. Not ever. And we'd better both keep that in mind. In just a few months he'll be wooing women across the ocean. Gone forever. This is strictly business, I am not his type and you and I are not to allow ourselves to get attached in any way. Period." So why did she feel as if she wanted to join Lightning and sit there waiting for tomorrow when Etienne would return?

Etienne lay back on the bed of his penthouse suite and tried not to think about a pair of worried caramel eyes. Why was he doing this? It was obvious that Meg Leighton wasn't exactly thrilled about going back to Fieldman's, and who could blame her? Her departure from the company had clearly been less than pleasant. Given what little he'd been able to glean about the Fieldman family, at least the sons, they had been users lacking not only business sense but also consciences.

He wondered why Alan Fieldman had fired Meg.

Not that it mattered. He could tell, just from their brief conversation and just by looking past her to her wildly decorated but thoughtful apartment and at the array of books on her shelves, that she had a brain and a desire to learn. The topics ranged from history to philosophy to various how-to books.

She obviously had gumption. She'd tried to keep him from steamrolling her. He felt a twinge of guilt at having used her friends' financial situation to convince her and wondered for a second if he was any better than Alan Fieldman.

Probably not. He knew his flaws and his shortcomings all too well. But he was different. He was going to do everything in his power to keep Meg and her friends from getting hurt. And he was going to do his very best to fulfill the promise he'd made to Meg to help her carve out her own place in the business community. When he left in a few months—and his whole goal was to do his work and move on to the next job—she and her friends would, he hoped, be happy and smiling.

At the word smiling, he thought of Meg's lips. She was a plain woman but her eyes and her lips were amazing. Just a slight twitch of those lips spoke volumes and called up unexpected heat in his body.

"Enough," he told himself. "You know the rules. You never get to stay. You never get to take anything away other than a brief respite from the pain and a sufficient amount of money to move on to the next project." Socializing with the subjects wasn't allowed. Ever.

CHAPTER TWO

"WHERE is everyone?" Meg asked as they entered Fieldman's Furnishings the next day.

Etienne looked around the big, empty office with weak sunlight filtering in through the streaked and dusty windows high overhead. It shone on the mottled blue carpeting that was worn thin in places. There was a crack in one of the walls, and despite the fact that people still worked here, the place smelled of neglect. "I gave them the day off," he said.

"Excuse me? You did what?" Meg turned to him, her brown eyes open wide. She was wearing some wild red and white thing that hid a lot of her body, but wasn't camouflage enough to hide the fact that she was shapely and generously curved.

He frowned at her reaction. "I sent them home. With pay," he clarified. "Don't worry, Meg. I didn't turn your friends out without compensating them."

Meg shook her head. "I didn't mean that. I wasn't accusing you of cheating Edie and the others. And I *know* this is *so* out of line, but I was just… The company is dying and you sent the workers home? Why would— I'm sorry for asking, but I just don't understand why you would do that."

He smiled suddenly. "Meg, see what a great help you're going to be. Look, you're already questioning my methods."

Instantly she looked contrite. A lovely pink crept up from the neckline of her white blouse. "Don't," he said suddenly. "There's no need to be embarrassed about the fact that you're questioning me. It's a good thing."

She frowned. "I'm not embarrassed."

"You're blushing."

"I never blush."

But she was. And in a very pretty way. The bloom continued to spread, the faint rose accenting the full curve of her cheeks. Etienne raised one brow. "Yes. You're blushing. If we're going to work together, we need truth between us."

Almost as if she couldn't help herself, Meg reached up and touched her face. The pale, almost indiscernible scar that ran three inches from the corner of her lip toward her ear was now the only part of her face that wasn't a delightful pink. There was something very… erotic about that small white scar, something that made a man think about placing his lips against that thin line and moving outward, kiss after kiss.

Etienne caught himself again and stopped that train of thought as quickly as he could. What on earth was wrong with him? The woman…Meg wasn't wearing anything vaguely suggestive. In fact, her clothing looked somewhat sacklike. Her shoes were made for comfort rather than to accentuate her legs. And yet he had been thinking…well never mind what he had been thinking. Or why. He didn't even want to know about the why. Instead he cleared his throat and flipped on a computer in the still, empty room. The sound of the machine booting up filled the silence. He looked at Meg.

"I *wasn't* lying or trying to be coy," she insisted. "I've never been a blusher."

"Good, then. It's something new in your life. These next few months are going to be all about new things. Unlike these out-of-date computers."

"You have a time frame?"

"I have a *goal*. Not only to bring back your business in the United States but to expand beyond your shores. There's a small business expo in Paris two months from now. Make an impression there and international business will flow in. That's our target date to be up and running again full speed."

"You're serious, aren't you? Two months seems so short. Not that I'm doubting you can do it. You're the genius of La Défense."

Etienne snapped to attention at Meg's mention of Paris's business district. "The genius of La Défense? And you surmised that how?"

"Um…you told me?" She looked up at him without guile, those big brown eyes as innocent as a newborn lamb's, even though he knew he had never told her the nickname given to him by the French press.

"Meg…" he drawled.

An instant expression of guilt shadowed her countenance. "All right, I looked you up on the Internet. I'm sorry if I intruded. I just… I don't really know you and I wanted to know if you were for real."

He wanted to smile at her forlorn tone. He felt very *real* staring at her right now, but…the Internet?

The urge to smile disappeared. He was from an old, well-known family. There had been articles written about Louisa's death. But that wasn't something he felt he could discuss. Despite the three years that had passed, the pain, the guilt was still like a flame inside him. "And what did you discover?" he asked, careful to keep his tone casual.

"I discovered that…you *are* real," she said simply, which said so much and so little at the same time. She hesitated. Then she took a deep breath. "So, can even a genius like you pull Fieldman's together in only two months? What can we accomplish in such a short time?"

Etienne felt a huge sense of relief. He wouldn't be asked to discuss Louisa. He wouldn't have to give evasive answers to mask his pain. If Meg had chanced upon that story, and she most likely had, she wasn't saying anything. For several long seconds he studied her carefully. She gazed back at him directly, unflinchingly. Only the way her fingers fidgeted with the cloth of her dress gave away even a hint of discomfort. All right, she probably knew his history. But she was ignoring it. He would, too, and he would be grateful. In other circumstances, he would be kissing her feet.

Which called up an image of something he knew he could never pursue.

"What can we do?" he asked, skirting all the issues except the only one he would allow himself. "Many things. When a company begins to fail, it's not enough to simply go back to the old ways. And yes, better accounting practices will help, but they won't get Fieldman's the attention we need to pique customers' curiosity. What we need are some quick, very visible, highly touted changes. We want a spark to intrigue the customers and fire up the employees. We want something to attract publicity."

He caught a smile on her face. "What?"

"I assume your changes won't be like the ones Alan made," she said.

Etienne laughed. "Well, I *was* thinking bunny rabbits. With carrots. Very eye-catching."

"Ah, I see you really *do* need me, after all," she said. "No bunny rabbits."

He tried to look wounded. "What do you suggest, then?"

For half a second, she looked self-conscious. Those pretty caramel eyes flew open wide. "All right, you don't want to go back to what Fieldman's was doing when Mary was in charge."

He slowly shook his head. "The world moves on. We have to move with it." It was a good reminder and more for himself than for Meg. He was a man constantly on the move, and he needed to be that way. There was no way to change the past. All he could do was move away from it.

"Your job takes you all around the world, doesn't it?"

"I never stop moving. It helps that I'm not married or likely to be. It wouldn't be fair to ask a woman to put up with a man like me who is never around."

Which was far more direct than he felt comfortable being, but he had learned that being direct was the only way.

Meg didn't even blink. In fact she smiled slightly. "I'm not a family woman, either, or likely to get married."

Which meant something bad had to have happened to her at some point.

"Someday I'll want children, but since I don't have them yet, I'm free to spend as much time on the job as necessary."

Children. Etienne's heart started thudding. He had once wanted a child.

He didn't speak. Memories rushed at him. A conversation with his wife. She hadn't wanted the baby. He had. But she was the one who lost her life due to the rigors of pregnancy and an undetected heart defect.

And he was obviously not hiding his reaction to her declaration well. Meg was looking at him with what could only be called concern in her expression. Etienne shook off the past. It was done. It was over. And he was making Meg nervous. That wasn't acceptable.

"But we don't need to spend time talking about my plans," she said quickly. "We need to discuss the company and…I understand what you said, but we don't want to toss out what worked completely, do we?" she asked. "That is, isn't my knowledge of what was working part of why you hired me?"

She licked her lips nervously. Etienne's pulse jumped. His body reacted…the way any man's body would react. And suddenly, standing here staring at those berry lips, he wondered for a second why he *had* hired Meg. She wasn't pretty in the common way at all—some might even call her plain—but there was something…some light in her eyes, something very full about those lips that made her very tempting, and temptation was never allowed to be a part of his dying business reclamation projects. Yet, here he was examining Meg as if he intended to do something that was out of the question.

He nearly swore. No doubt he'd simply been depriving himself of female companionship for too long. He was clearly going to have to watch himself around Meg Leighton. And she was still waiting for an answer to her question.

"Yes, you have the keys to what made Fieldman's work before. Let's take that and give it a twist."

"Something classic but fresh," she said.

"Fresh and enticing," he agreed.

"Maybe…" Her whole face lit up.

"What?" He watched her, but she suddenly looked self-conscious.

"No. Maybe I'd better let that idea sink in and think it through a bit, let it play out and mature before I share it. I have an awful and long-standing tendency to jump in and do things without waiting for common sense to kick in, to react or speak without thinking. Bad habit."

"Not always."

She gave him a look that said he was clearly wrong. "For me it is. That's part of what I want you to help me with. How to think on my feet without saying or doing something tremendously terrible or embarrassing."

"What kinds of things have you said and done?"

She shook her head. "No. I am so *not* sharing my most embarrassing moments. It's bad enough that they happened in the first place. I've taken numerous classes to improve myself. I've tried to learn how to ski, how to skate, how to enter a room, and I know the basic concepts. I've even been taught how to fall gracefully several times, but when it comes down to the wire, I'm still the person who steps on the banana peel and ends up in an embarrassing heap with absolutely no grace. Or the one who yells something loud and embarrassing just as everyone in the room stops talking. I live in fear that someone will catch me on a camera phone and I'll end up on the Internet as one of those 'most watched videos.'" She threw out one hand in a gesture of remorse. "You don't happen to carry a camera phone around with you, do you?"

Etienne couldn't stop himself from chuckling. "Yes, I do, but I would never use it against you, Meg. That would be *trop*...I mean *too* unfeeling of me."

She gave him another look. "Ah, so you're a gentleman. Not the type of man I meet every day." Which made him wonder what her experiences with men had been. "So...about that idea for the company... How do you feel about leather?"

Etienne nearly choked. Ah, her so-called habit of saying something without thinking about how her audience would hear it...now he understood a little bit. Still, in this case, it was a charming addition to her personality. This woman was a delight, was all he could think of. Despite her original reluctance to work with him, she had clearly jumped in with both feet now that she'd made up her mind to commit. "Leather?" he asked, reminding himself that she was talking about furniture, not something kinky. "I like leather. What man doesn't?"

"All right. I'll keep that in mind. Tomorrow I'll bring you ten ideas."

"Of ways to use leather creatively."

They had been moving deeper into the office, but now she stopped and faced him. Though her eyes only met his chin, she tipped her head back and gave him the kind of look a woman gave to an errant schoolboy. "Are you making fun of me, Etienne?"

No. He was enjoying her. Immensely. In a quite improper way that he knew darn well he was going to regret. Later. "I might be," he conceded. "But I mean it only in the very best way. I think you're unique. I like the way your thought process works." And that, he suddenly realized was the key to Fieldman's future success. There was always a key.

Finding it was the challenge. And here she was, standing right beside him. The woman who was going to make the difference in a way that hadn't occurred to him earlier.

"What?" she said. "Why are you looking at me that way?"

"What way?"

"I don't know. As if… I don't know. You're smiling. A lot. And I know I didn't even say anything remotely funny or weird. At least not this time. Did I—have I torn something again?" She looked down at her blouse, fussing with the material, clearly embarrassed.

Oh, yes, Meg was definitely it. But he didn't want to frighten her or to make her think that he was looking at her in a suggestive way. That wasn't fair. He was very careful not to even hint that he was offering things he wasn't offering or that he wanted things he couldn't be allowed to want.

"It's nothing overt you've done. I've just come up with a new part of our plan, the most important part."

"Wonderful. What is it?"

"You."

She shook her head. "I don't understand. I'm already here."

"No, not like this. Fieldman's needs to be fresh, different, exciting. You asked me yesterday to take you on as a student of sorts. So, let's do that. In a major way. Let's make you the new face of Fieldman's."

If he had taken her to a horror movie, Etienne could not have surprised a more shocked and terrified look on Meg's face. "That is so not going to happen," she said. "That would be such a mistake."

"No. It's not a mistake. Meg, look at me."

She looked, and those big beautiful, terrified eyes nearly tore his heart out.

"I'm not going to hurt you," he said, but she looked as if she didn't believe him. "I wouldn't do that. Believe me, I've hurt people in my life and it's not the kind of thing I want to repeat. Ever."

"You don't know what you're asking me. You want me to stand up in front of people."

"I do. I want you to be the new symbol for the company."

"I can't do that. I have 'being the center of attention' issues."

Somehow he refrained from smiling. She really was frightened.

"Any other kinds of issues?"

"Trust."

"I have trust issues, too."

"You do?"

"Yes. I try not to ask people to trust me, and I'm not going to do that now, but I will tell you this. I won't send you out to speak or have your picture taken unless I'm right there with you. I'll be there to guide you and to shield you. And if anything happens that you don't like, I'll whisk you right out of there."

"Even if it hurts Fieldman's?"

"Even then."

She took a deep breath. "And you think this will help the company."

"There aren't any guarantees, Meg, but I know this much. A personality always gets more attention than a piece of furniture ever will. Mary was, I understand, a personality, and half the reason people bought from Fieldman's. We need someone to take her place, and you fit the bill perfectly, especially since you were Mary's protégée. If Fieldman's is going to rise again and to succeed, you're the best bet we have."

She hesitated, but only for a second. "All right, if you think it will help the people here, I'm in. I'll consider it my duty."

Etienne nearly groaned at her choice of words. "Don't do it for duty. That's something you do because you feel you have to. It robs you of your control and your joy and in the end may leave you with nothing." Which he knew better than anyone.

And which was obviously saying too much. Meg Leighton was studying him carefully, possibly seeing damaged parts of his soul that he didn't want exposed.

"Consider your spokesperson role to be part of our agreement. On the job training," he suggested.

She blew out a breath. "Okay, all right. Yes. So… what do we do now?"

"We get started."

"On me?"

Such guileless eyes. No wonder she had trust issues. Some wolf could waltz right past her defenses and hurt her. But it wouldn't be him.

"Let's start with the building first," he said. "Show me everything you know."

If he concentrated on the building, he would be less distracted by the woman. It was a solid theory. But as he walked behind her, the soft sound of her voice, the sway of her hips, even the gentle line of her arm as she pointed out the details of their surroundings…mesmerized him.

Etienne frowned, angry at his completely inappropriate reaction. He reminded himself of why he had come here and what the rules were. No attachments, no touching.

Suddenly Meg stopped. She turned and sighed. "The state of this place, the books… Saving the company is going to be a challenge, isn't it?" she asked, those big brown eyes worried.

"Don't worry, I can handle it," he said, the promise as much about his reaction to the woman as it was to the company. He was *not* going to get close enough to risk hurting her.

"You're very confident, aren't you?" she asked with a smile that sent pleasure arcing through him.

"No. I'm determined," he said. Determined to do what he had come to do and then leave. And that meant ignoring the fact that what he wanted right this minute was to see her smile again. No, if he was truly honest with himself, he wanted more. He wanted to taste her.

And for the first time he realized just how difficult it was going to be, working with Meg. Her smile, her lips… The woman was going to be a major distraction.

CHAPTER THREE

It HAD been a long day. Meg and Etienne had covered every inch of the building. They'd pored over paperwork, gone through the computer files, sifted through the desk drawers that Alan Fieldman had left behind. There was a photo of Meg in there that she had given him. There was also a photo of Paula Avery, the stunningly attractive but uninformed woman Alan had hired and then promoted over Meg three weeks later. And even photos of two other women, one somewhat scantily clad.

Meg had discovered these while Etienne was busy elsewhere, and now she quickly shoved all the photos deep in the drawer and closed it. She had been fooled by Alan. He had seen that she had been his mother's favorite and had used her to make points with Mary. The fact that Meg had fallen for his act, had allowed her defenses to fall that much…it was a pathetic chapter in her life she wanted to remain closed. And she was wiser now. She would not allow herself to be weak again.

Especially not with Etienne. That thought dropped in out of nowhere but she didn't turn away. He had made a point of mentioning that he wasn't in the market for romantic entanglements. Some women might be offended, but Meg was glad for the gentle warning. The truth might sting, but it was always better than a lie. And she had learned the dangers of lying to herself. Etienne was not and never would be for her.

"All right, we know the lay of the land now, Meg," Etienne was saying, causing her to start.

She pulled herself back into the here and now and the business at hand. "The situation at Fieldman's looks pretty desperate," she said.

"Getting cold feet?"

She was. The thought of holding people's lives in her hands filled her with dread. She'd spoken with Edie at lunchtime, and her friend was so scared she was practically in tears.

"I don't want my friends to suffer," she said. "Edie's husband got laid off from his job last year and he hasn't been able to find another one. This place is all she has. She's not the only one, either. The people here…they're good people."

"They didn't stand up to Alan when he fired you."

"They have children, dependents. I don't. And I don't blame them. What could they have said that would have made a difference? And anyway, my problems with Alan were of my own making."

Etienne swore at that. At least she assumed he was swearing. "I don't know those words," she told him.

"Good. And you're not going to, either, *ma chère*."

Meg felt a jolt, a warmth, go through her at the French phrase. All right, she'd had high school French, enough to realize that he meant it just as a friendly term, but coming from Etienne's lips…oh darn, Etienne could say the words peanut butter and a woman would go all gooey inside.

Except me, she thought. I just declared my intent to be strong not two minutes ago. And it's true. It's got to be true. I have to make it true. Etienne's not available. I'm not available and I don't want to be available. From now on I'm immune to Etienne. Please let me be immune. Don't let me do or say something stupid.

"This Alan...he was the one in the wrong. You shouldn't let a man like that dictate your life," Etienne told her. "Your worth should never be dependent on one person." He said the words angrily with a slash of his hand.

"I don't let my worth depend on the opinion of others," she assured him. "I won't." But she had. Once upon a time she had tried to break past her parents' conviction that her birth had intruded on their plans and ruined their lives, but she hadn't been able to do that, and now that no longer mattered. She had a goal and a purpose and none of what had happened in her past could stop her.

"Good. I'm glad to hear that," Etienne said with a smile that lit up those sexy, silvery-blue eyes. "We'll save your friends together, Meg. This won't be all on your head. I wouldn't allow you to carry that burden or to ever feel that you were solely responsible for saving another person. I would never have asked you to go through anything like that alone." He broke off abruptly and she wondered what his experience with burdens or trying to save people had been, but she'd read the online articles about him losing his wife and baby and she was sure he knew about the depths of despair and the fear of not being able to save someone. He had good reason to travel the world alone and keep his heart intact.

Meg's eyes felt suddenly misty. She blinked. "Thank you."

"Still," he said in that low, deep voice of his, "I have

to express my admiration. You were amazingly adept at deciphering those ledgers. They were gibberish to me, and I've looked at more than my share of ledgers."

She shrugged. "Mary had her own system. In retrospect, it probably wasn't a great idea."

"So, the ledgers are translated. That's one bridge crossed," he said. "Now, on to the next."

She blinked. They had already been here for ten hours. "What's next?"

"You," he said.

"Me?" Her heartbeat went into overdrive.

"I made you a promise yesterday. We had a deal."

"Oh. Me. You're going to transform me. And you're going to make me into a worthy spokesperson."

"You're already worthy and you don't need transforming. You need polish."

"Lots of polish."

He frowned, but she ignored that. "What are you going to teach me first?"

She looked up at him and was surprised to see a look of intense heat in his eyes. "First I'm going to dress you."

Meg swallowed hard. Even though, she reminded herself, there was no reason to be self-conscious. Dressing a woman was a lot different from undressing her. But her appearance was the last thing she had envisioned when she'd asked Etienne to help make her a success. This was unsettling, unnerving. The very thought… She felt ridiculously frivolous, but somehow she was sure that Etienne had encountered any number of successful women in his life. He knew the right ingredients.

"All right," she said slowly. "I suppose you could do that. I was never very fond of this dress, anyway."

"That dress should be destroyed so that no one can ever wear it again."

He sounded so offended that she just had to smile. "That's going a bit far, isn't it?"

"Not nearly far enough, Meg. You have...curves. You should show them."

"Curves?" she said with a laugh and a shake of her head. "Well, thank you for putting it that way instead of simply saying that I weigh too much."

"You do not weigh too much. You have shape. Here," he said, motioning toward her breast. He didn't touch her at all, but she felt as if she had been touched. "And here," he continued, curving his palm near her hip.

With great effort, Meg continued to breathe.

"Shape is a good thing," Etienne said. *"N'est ce pas? Isn't it?"*

It had never been a good thing for her before, but...

"You know a lot about women and what makes them...noticeable, don't you? That is, noticeable in a good way, not in a bad way."

"Has someone been making you feel bad about your looks?"

Okay, that was a subject she was not going to discuss. Doing so would only make her look as if she felt sorry for herself, and she refused to be that kind of whining woman. "No. Not at all," she said brightly.

He smiled, and she knew that he probably suspected she was lying. "Good, because you should be proud of your looks. You have..."

He was hesitating. In her Meg plow-ahead way, she wanted to help, but discussing her physical attributes was virgin territory for her and also incredibly dangerous to her peace of mind, she thought, remembering that curving-his-hands-near-her-body exploration that had made her ache and want to squirm closer. "Etienne, I'm not some fragile flower. You don't have to be so careful with me. I'm comfortable with who I am and I want you to know that I can do a pretty decent job of camouflaging this scar with makeup when I take the time to do that if it will help my image," she offered, gesturing toward her mouth.

"Yes. I noticed that enchanting scar, Meg," he said. And somehow the way he said it, he made it sound as if every woman on earth should only *wish* they had such a scar. "How did you get it?"

But that was another topic she didn't care to discuss in great depth. "It was just a little fall. Not a big deal," she said, though of course it had felt like a very big deal when she was growing up. Her mother had constantly urged her to cover it up and had bemoaned the fact that Meg would never be half as beautiful as her sister, Ann. Ann being the grown daughter Leslie Leighton and her husband had actually planned and wanted and cherished, not the daughter who had been a major mistake, who had come along late in their lives and who had trapped them into staying in a marriage they wanted to rid themselves of. "And anyway, it happened so long ago that the details no longer matter."

And with this gorgeous, exotic, successful man gazing at her face as if he would like to touch her, Meg couldn't stay focused on the details, anyway.

She struggled to clear her head and concentrate on what they had been talking about before this disconcerting discussion of her scar began. "Since you're new to the area, you probably don't know any shops we can go to, so I'll help," she said and she offered up a few of the ones she frequented: inexpensive little out-of-the-way shops.

"I was thinking more…classic with maybe a hint of sass thrown in." He rattled off the names of several upscale stores and boutiques in the area.

Meg raised her brows in astonishment. "You live in Paris. So, how do you know these things? Where women buy their clothes and what the best places are?" she asked.

"It's part of the job."

"You dress women often?"

"Sometimes out-of-town clients have emergencies. It's a good rule of thumb, wherever you are, to always know a few good restaurants, a few good theaters and places where both women and men can pick up emergency supplies. It shows your clients that you're prepared to go the extra mile to help them. Presentation is important."

"I'll remember that, but…"

He waited.

"I can't afford to shop at those places."

"Yes, you can. I'm paying you very well." He threw out a figure that made Meg's breath catch in her throat.

"That's far too much. I assumed you were going to pay me what Alan's former assistant was making, or at least something in the ballpark."

He smiled. Okay, she was being pushy and outspoken again, but still…

"It's not too much," he said. "And you're going to earn every penny. You're now Fieldman's. When people see Fieldman's Furnishings, what they're really going to see is Meg Leighton. Here and abroad."

Her courage nearly faltered at that. Having people

staring at her had always been difficult. But she had asked for his help and he was going to help her. She had agreed to be the spokesperson only hours ago. She couldn't turn craven on him now. "And as the actual owner of Fieldman's, you'll be in the spotlight, too."

"Yes, but I'm used to it. I've lived in that kind of spotlight all my life. You haven't. That means you need ways to conquer stage fright, should it rear its ugly head. You need the right clothes and you need to be able to make an instant impression. Consider it part of your job description."

"All right. But when I said that I wanted you to help me be a success, I wasn't even thinking that you would clothe me."

"What were you thinking I would do?"

"Teach me."

"I will."

"Guide me," she said, her voice coming out a little whispery and very unlike herself.

"I promise I'll do that and more."

Meg didn't even want to try to imagine what the *and more* part meant. Instead she followed Etienne out into the sunlight, into his sleek, expensive car and, eventually, into a very expensive boutique that she had only ever seen from the outside.

"We need a wardrobe," he told the woman. "Only items that complement Meg's complexion and her figure. Nothing gaudy, but…think…"

He studied Meg. "Nothing drab, either. Meg likes bright colors."

"How do you know that?" Meg asked.

"I peeked in your doorway while we were talking yesterday. Your living room is quite out of the ordinary."

She laughed. "You're being quite polite by describing it that way. Even Edie tells me I went too far with the aqua and tangerine and yellow."

"Maybe, but it suits you. And all those colors complement your eyes."

"My eyes are plain brown."

He did that wicked eyebrow raising thing again. "You, *mademoiselle*, don't even know what color your eyes are. There's nothing plain about them."

While he was talking he was looking into her eyes just as if they were alone. But they weren't, and Meg felt suddenly self-conscious. The saleswoman probably thought that Meg was paying Etienne for his services or something. He could certainly spend his time with someone totally beautiful if he wanted to.

"Okay, my eyes are gorgeous," she lied. "What should I buy?"

"This," he said, pointing out a stunning camel colored suit and adding a melon silk blouse. "For starters."

And he meant what he said. For the next hour, Meg tried on outfit after outfit. Etienne nixed many of them. "That doesn't do justice to her legs," he'd say, just as if Meg's legs had ever been the kind of thing anyone admired. And yet…in the camel suit or in the knee skimming navy sheath with subtle red trim, wearing red pumps that were slightly higher than she was used to, her legs did look different. Thinner.

"You have an eye," the saleswoman said to Etienne, and Meg knew that the woman was wishing that she was the woman Etienne was with.

It's just business, Meg wanted to tell her. We're not romantic people. We're just on this outing as part of the deal we made and because we need to make an impression at the expo. Still, the woman was right. Etienne had obviously dressed many women before, and those women had undoubtedly had more polish than the average female. It was a good thing to keep in mind. Even if he had the time and inclination to get involved with someone during his stay in Chicago, he was not for someone like Meg Leighton.

"Not this," Meg said when Etienne handed her a slender black strapless dress. "I'm all about business. I won't need anything this formal."

"Oh, yes," he said. "There will be at least one event either here or in Paris where you'll need this. I'm sure of it."

Suddenly fear took hold of her. What was she doing? She, plain, always awkward Meg Leighton, the girl whose mother had accidentally scarred her, then reminded Meg again and again over the years that she would never go far if she didn't cover up her deformity, lose weight, stand up taller, remake herself into a completely different person, was here trying on a cocktail dress just as if she was actually going to wear it.

She frowned and started to put it back.

Etienne gave the saleswoman a look, sending her scurrying away. He placed a hand on Meg's arm, and sensation jolted through her. Heat suffused her body.

"Please, Meg, do this," Etienne said, leaning closer to her so that she nearly had to close her eyes from the sheer sensation of feeling the warmth of his body. "You need to do this. Alan was an idiot."

Her eyes flew open at that. "What?"

"Don't you think that I know that that…that fool sapped your confidence in yourself when he let you go?"

"I never had that kind of total confidence in myself.

Well, other than my brains. I knew I had those, but this…my…person…"

His eyes opened wide. "You should have confidence here, too. Look at you, Meg," he said, turning her so that they both faced the mirror. "Look at your cheekbones." Standing behind her, he raised his arms, framing her body so that his fingertips skimmed her skin.

Her heart nearly flipped over. "I—I have that scar," she reminded him.

"Yes, and I explained how adorable and sexy that was."

"I think you're blind."

"I have twenty-twenty vision."

If she hadn't been so overwhelmed by his nearness, she might have laughed at how seriously he had taken her comment. As it was, she could barely breathe.

"Think of you in this dress," he said. "With your hair up like this." He reached down and gently lifted her long hair, so that her neck was exposed.

And then he simply stared.

"What?" she asked. "What's wrong?" She tried to twist.

"You have a beautiful neck. Has anyone ever told you that?"

And then the sheer incongruity of the situation hit Meg. The nervous laughter bubbled up out of her.

"I said something funny?" he asked.

"You said something wonderful. Not true, but wonderful. I definitely have to start hanging around with a whole lot more Frenchmen. Are they all like you?"

She looked in the mirror, and saw that his eyes were dark and not at all happy. "A few compliments. *True* compliments," he insisted. "And you want to start meeting all the men in Paris. And…how *am* I?"

Meg frowned, confused.

"You asked if they were all like me. What did you mean?"

"Only that you were full of pretty talk."

"*Pretty* talk?"

"You know, that thing about my neck. As if my neck is any different from any other woman's neck."

"You," he said. "Need more than just business lessons. You need to be introduced to the right kind of men. Obviously someone was negligent in your upbringing if no one has told you these things."

She shook her head, sadly. "My parents were…not nice parents, but they weren't the only ones. Fat little girls with scars on their faces do not get compliments on anything other than their brains. And even then, pretty girls with brains still win."

"Well, this time you'll be the one to win. And you are pretty," he told her, clearly more than a bit angry.

"Please send all these things here," Etienne told the saleswoman as he gave her his credit card and a slip of paper with Meg's address on it. "And she'll need underthings. Lots of them. Silky, pretty stuff. Meg…"

But Meg was suddenly blushing horribly and by now even she knew that she was blushing for real. "You're not buying me lingerie," she said. "I'm not that kind of woman."

"What kind is that? Do you mean you don't wear underwear, Meg?"

Meg heard the woman make a choking sound and she wasn't sure if the lady was trying to hold back a laugh or just as startled as Meg was.

Meg looked at Etienne and there was no question that he was laughing. He was trying to cow her into buying something she truly didn't need.

"Sometimes I don't," she said, blustering in and lifting her chin defiantly even though it was a lie. She didn't care. All this talk of how pretty she was… How could she have forgotten her rotten luck with men? Alan had told her all kinds of lies and she had believed them. They hadn't been nearly as preposterous as the things Etienne had been saying.

But she took one look at Etienne and knew that she had stepped over a line. His eyes were dark and heated, and the look on his face was…territorial, sensual, utterly male.

There was no way she knew anything at all about handling that kind of reaction. She'd never elicited that kind of reaction from any man. She was definitely in over her head.

"But I'll probably need some things for the times I do wear underwear," she said quickly. "I'll tell you my size," she told the woman, scrambling for a scrap of paper. She was so not going to say her bra size out loud. Especially not in Etienne's presence.

She handed the woman the paper and began a march toward the door. Every step she took was agony. She felt as if the eyes of the world were on her, and that she was alone. It was a feeling she knew all too well.

But within seconds Etienne was beside her. He took her arm and curled his hand around hers. "I'm sorry," he said.

"For what?"

"I embarrassed you."

And she realized something. "You weren't laughing at me, were you?"

"I was teasing you. Because we're… Because I like you. That's a very different thing from laughing at someone."

Warmth stole through Meg. He was right, so right, but she had never had that. That closeness. At least not with a man.

"That *was* pretty clever and amusing," she conceded. "At least after I get over my initial surprise. Did you see that poor woman's face? We must have shocked her."

"She thinks we're sleeping together," he said. "Or at least she did until you told me that you don't wear underwear. A man who was sleeping with a woman would know that."

Her delight in their closeness dimmed a bit. She and Etienne would be friends but despite the way he affected her, they could and would never be more.

Still, she'd known that from the start. She had no right at all to complain. As it was, his comment reminded her of why they had been arguing. "Etienne, why *do* I need special underwear? No one but me will ever see it."

"A shame," he said, "if that's true. But, even so, you need to feel beautiful all the way to your skin. In fact, Meg, I've learned a few things about you today. Your instruction has to be far more thorough than I had originally planned. We're not only going to resurrect Fieldman's Furnishings in the next two months, but by the time you and I are through, you're going to know that you're an attractive woman right down to the cellular level. Men will fall at your feet. Women will admire and envy you."

She laughed at his ridiculously optimistic comments, but later when he was seeing her off at her door, Meg had to face reality. Etienne had come into her life like a shooting star. He was all fire and enthusiasm and confidence, but she wasn't that way.

Picking up Lightning, who uncharacteristically allowed herself the indignity, Meg looked up at Etienne. "Do you always have this much passion about everything?"

"What do you mean?"

"I mean…me. I know I asked for help, and I know I need to look right if I'm supposed to be a spokesperson, but you've jumped in and taken me on as a kind of project, one where you're determined to get the blue ribbon by turning me into the best jam at the county fair. You're so sure, so enthusiastic, so determined. Don't you ever doubt? Or question?"

He reached out one hand, and Lightning coyly batted his finger with her paw. "I question many things," he said solemnly. "More than you'll ever know. I make lots of mistakes and I hate that. I've done things I regret and even things I can't live with. I question myself every day about those things and I always will, but I don't question truth when it stares me in the face, Meg. You are an amazing, striking woman."

"And you know this how?"

He smiled gently and tucked one finger under her chin. Lightning made her escape. "I know this because you came back to the business, you did something you hated the thought of doing just to save your friends. And I know this because I'm a man, and I have eyes in my head."

And without another word, he leaned over and placed his lips on hers. Gently but firmly, he kissed her. And then he left.

Meg felt as if her knees had turned to noodles. She swayed on her feet, but she didn't move.

"I'll see you in the morning, Meg," Etienne called to her as he exited the building. "Tomorrow we pick up the pace."

But as she lay in her bed that night Meg wondered if she could take a faster pace with Etienne. Already, she was short of breath and not thinking clearly. Another day like this and she wouldn't be able to survive.

Her mind was playing dangerous tricks on her. Her lips were tingling, and she was most certainly wanting things that she could never, ever have.

Drat the man! Why couldn't he have stayed in France?

Because Edie would be destroyed. He had to come save Edie. And Meg had to help.

But, Meg wondered, who would save *her* when Etienne had gone back to France and all she had were aching lips and arms and memories. She was just going to have to be stronger and more resilient tomorrow. She was definitely going to have to stop acting like a total idiot and wondering what it would be like if Etienne kissed her again.

CHAPTER FOUR

ETIENNE filed past the row of people at their desks. He had opened the doors to the employees today, and they were all waiting for him to say something. The expressions on their faces were a mixture of fervent hope and something less than pleasant. Suspicion. Well, that was to be expected. They didn't know him. Their fates were in his hands.

But when Meg strolled in a few minutes behind him, there were no conflicting emotions flickering across people's faces. Everyone was smiling. Tiny, wiry little Edie went to Meg and hugged her. "Welcome home," the older woman said.

And then there was a round of applause as others joined in, calling out greetings. Meg waved to her friends and the room went unexpectedly quiet. In the second immediately afterward, Etienne heard a man in the back of the room mutter something about how he hoped the new owner wouldn't lie to Meg like Alan had, followed by someone else's quick shushing sound.

Meg looked momentarily nonplussed, and Edie, with a wide, obviously hastily pasted on and slightly nervous smile, turned to Etienne. "We're very glad you bought the place, Mr. Gavard. I'm sure you'll be a good employer and treat all of us well." She looked toward the corner where the comment had come from and where an older man was looking decidedly uncomfortable and trying to pretend that he was fiddling with the copy machine. Etienne would have wanted to laugh except for the fact that the word "lie" had been used. He'd been told that Alan had fired Meg. Lying was something else entirely.

"I'm going to do my best by *all* of you," Etienne told the group. "And…um…no lying."

Meg rolled her eyes.

"Don't let them push you around," she told him.

Now everyone looked shocked. Etienne couldn't help it. One corner of his mouth lifted, even though he fought the urge.

"She's giving him orders," someone whispered.

"I'm just… Oh, never mind," Meg said and she headed back toward the inner office where she and Etienne had been working yesterday. Etienne noticed that she was wearing a navy-blue suit that fit her body, emphasizing the gentle sway of her hips as she moved.

Heat—and admiration for what she'd tried to do for him—filtered into his consciousness. He remembered how soft her lips had been and how her eyes had widened in shock when he'd kissed her. She had said nothing then, but today she'd found her voice again. Good.

"Meg's quite a sassy one, isn't she?" Etienne remarked half to himself. It seemed he liked sass.

"But very nice," the old man in the corner said.

"I've noticed," Etienne agreed.

The man looked mollified.

"Do you need anything special of us, Mr. Gavard?"

Edie asked. "We know the company is in very bad shape. Mr. Fieldman wouldn't have run if that weren't the case, because he wanted this place badly enough to do whatever it took to get his mother to leave it to him."

She frowned, and Etienne began to suspect just how deep the problem with Alan had gone. Besides the man's general ignorance of good business, his blindness to his employees' talents and his lack of common sense, Alan Fieldman must have done something to Meg beyond firing her. No wonder the man in the corner was concerned.

Etienne looked at Edie's aging face and the fervent, anxious expression in her eyes. "I want you all to trust me. I know that's asking a lot. This is your work, your identity, your livelihood. But I want you to know that I don't take that lightly. My sole aim in coming here is to turn this place around."

"To make it profitable," Edie said.

"Yes." Even though he had little interest in his own profit in this case. He didn't really need the money. He needed the sanity and the peace of mind.

"If I don't do that, I will have failed, and I don't like failure. So, for now, what I want is for you to have faith, to keep doing your jobs as well as you can, to follow whatever instructions Meg and I give you and above all to squelch any rumors that Fieldman's is failing. That can be disastrous in the business world. From this moment on, we're on the path to success, and we want the world to know that."

"So…we're not failing?" an older woman asked. She was standing next to a desk that had a nameplate that read Marie. The nearly worshipful naked hope on Marie's expression almost buckled Etienne's knees. His life had nearly been ruined by people expecting too much of him, he had unwittingly but callously sacrificed his wife to the expectations of his family, his name and position, and here he was *intentionally* seeking out those who had no choice but to put their lives in his hands. So why did he choose to do this in his work?

Because I have to, he reminded himself. He had to be able to live with himself. A little, at least.

"From now on we're a team, and this team is going to survive," he told them. "I'll need all of your help. I may be asking you to do things that haven't been asked of you before. Legal things," he said at the look of alarm in one man's eyes. "But we're cutting corners to make things profitable and we may all have to pitch in and do double duty at times when people are sick or have emergencies. No temporary workers to step in, no outsiders handling maintenance. This is all going to be…us. Our methods may be a bit unconventional, but from here on out you have a vested interest in making sure this company succeeds. If it does, it's going to be yours someday. This will become an employee-owned company."

A buzzing began through the room. One person stepped forward. "Does that mean we can fire you if we don't like what you're doing?"

Etienne did laugh then. "Not yet. Besides, you won't have to fire me. When things are back in shape here, I'll be gone. Until then, you're going to be my prime concern, and I'll expect complete cooperation. This isn't going to be easy."

"What about Meg?" someone asked. "Where will she be when we're going full tilt again?"

Etienne didn't know. For some reason that bothered him even though it shouldn't. Meg was charming, but she was temporary, as was everyone in his life. Holding people at a distance was how he had maintained his sanity these past few years. "Meg will be wherever she wishes," he said. But he couldn't help wondering where that would be.

Meg bent over the desk beside Etienne. They were discussing changes to the line, how positions in the firm would have to be altered to accommodate the current financial situation and all the details of what they needed to do to bring life back to the business.

"I especially like this one," he said, pointing to one of her ideas for a new line of sofas. "I've contacted a textile firm in the east that's willing to cut their price if we give their firm prominent billing in our presentations and ads. As soon as we have some mockups and photos, we're going to schedule you with the photographer and visit some trade fairs. We'll speak to the local press."

Meg froze. Her heart began to thud wildly. She looked directly into his eyes. He gazed back at her, reached out and tilted her chin up gently.

"I once knew a woman who was totally dependent on a man for her identity and for her…everything. That won't be you. You'll have no need of a man if you don't want one, because you'll have you. You'll have this," he said, gesturing toward the room. "I can help you get from here to there. I want to. Let me."

His voice was like a caress. Meg almost felt herself sway toward him, but that would be a mistake, one neither of them wanted.

She nodded. "Thank you," she said softly. "I made the rounds and have started to draft some revised job descriptions so we can take up the slack in areas where we've been lacking due to letting our outside services go."

"Good. But I want everyone to know that they'll be paid extra," Etienne said. "I'm not a poor man and I've set aside funds for the restructuring of Fieldman's."

"Thank you. Some of them have been here most of their careers. This is a second home for them." And for some like me, she thought, it was more than a home. It was a haven. Or at least it had been, before the incident with Alan.

"They love you," he said simply, and she glanced up into his eyes.

"They know me."

"It's more than that."

Meg shrugged. "I tend to get a little territorial and protective about people I care about. They know that."

"Sounds like they reciprocate. Some of them are very concerned about how I'm going to treat you."

She took a deep breath and reached for a jar that held pencils. Cupping her hands around it she pondered how much she wanted to divulge.

"I'll talk to them about that," she said. "They shouldn't be speaking to you that way."

He reached out and placed his hand on her arm. Sensation shot through her, awareness of the man beside her nearly overwhelmed her, warmth and something more made her feel flushed and awkward and needy and…

She lost her grip on the cup, and pens and pencils tumbled out, rolling off the desk.

She lurched to grab them, but Etienne's grip was gentle but firm. "Leave them, Meg. And…don't speak to the others about how you want them to treat me. I have to form my own relationship with them. I'm capable of doing that. What I'm not capable of is reading minds. I think I need to know more of what happened here before you left. As it is, I seem to be the only one in the dark."

"It doesn't matter."

"It does. It affects how everyone thinks of you and me. It affects how you approach your work."

"I wouldn't cheat you of my time or effort, not after we made a deal!"

"I know that, but you might be too careful, too controlled."

"That's not such a bad thing. I've been meaning to work on that self-control all my life."

He smiled then. "Self-control has its time and place. Not yelling at your employer is a good example of self-control."

"I haven't yelled at you."

"You've lectured me," he teased. "You told me not to let the employees talk to me in a disrespectful manner, and right in front of them, too."

"That was bad," she agreed, but she couldn't seem to keep from smiling.

"It was," he said, but he chuckled when he said it.

"Okay, reminding myself not to try to protect you from Raymond, the man at the copier, is a good example of self-control. What's a *bad* example of self-control?" she asked.

"Not voicing your opinions or offering your ideas because you think they might be seen as too wild and crazy or that others might criticize you or make fun of you."

She grew solemn then. "That's a tough one. I'll have to think about it."

"Did Alan criticize your ideas?"

So…they *were* going to discuss Alan.

"Why do you say that?"

"Your friends… They're worried about you because of Alan. I can understand that, because you told me that he fired you. But, what I can't understand is why."

Oh, no. She so didn't want to do this.

"He wanted me gone."

"Obviously." Etienne waited.

Meg stubbornly decided to dig in her heels. "These things happen."

"No." Etienne slowly shook his head. "I've run many companies, had thousands of employees, but…look at your work," he said, gesturing to the mock-ups she'd made in the middle of the night last night. "You told me you would come up with ten good ideas and you did it in a matter of hours. They're good ideas, and you mapped out the pros and cons of each one. You suggested possible options for changes. You circulated among the employees and thought up new ways to make things run more efficiently. You understand Mary's obscure accounting procedures. You know this company inside and out. You should be the last person standing if this company should go down, not the one who gets kicked out. What happened here, Meg? I can't be in the dark."

"Is that the only reason you need to know?"

"No, it's not. I don't like seeing people mistreated. I also don't like asking this of you, and ordinarily I wouldn't pry, but you were the brains of this company and Alan was the owner. You were asked to leave. I'm trying to piece this company back together, and if there are secrets or undercurrents that are still in place, then…"

"There aren't any undercurrents. They ended the day Alan asked me to leave." Meg closed her eyes. Tightly. "But yes, there were undercurrents prior to that. Alan and his brother had nothing to do with Fieldman's when they were younger, but three years ago, after they had both been out in the world for a while, they came back and joined the company. Alan was more outgoing, more take charge. He…he paid attention to me and eventually we became involved. He gave me a ring, but we didn't set a date even though we'd been engaged for a long time. Then Mary died and she left the company to him. His brother left immediately. And soon after that, Alan hired a new woman, promoted her over me and fired me. I had served my purpose."

"You're saying he pursued you only because Mary loved you."

"Yes. Because I was Mary's favorite employee, marrying me became his ticket to the CEO position. But I hadn't realized that he was simply using me to beat out his brother for the position. I had no idea there was a contest going on."

Etienne swore in French and then he swore some more. "No wonder your friends warned me. I'm surprised they didn't do more. Had I been in their shoes I would have."

"You're not to blame for my ignorance."

Etienne swore again.

"Stop swearing," she told him.

"I wasn't."

"It doesn't matter. I don't know French, so you could have been saying 'Pass the pretzels' for all I know, but it *sounded* very much like swearing, so it's the same difference."

"Then I apologize, but, Meg…you have to know that you weren't the one at fault here. The man was and is an ass. He didn't deserve you."

"Nonetheless I was going to marry him and now I'm

not. End of story. It's over. It's ancient history. I'm completely fine now."

Except of course she wasn't completely fine. A woman like her, one who had faced rejection and untrustworthy people all her childhood and who had thought she had finally managed to make a place for herself using only her wits, didn't easily get over the shock of knowing she'd fallen victim to a con man. She had given Alan her heart and her trust and had been made to look like a naive fool.

"I hope when we're done here that you'll be able to tell Alan Fieldman that you've won. Sometimes men aren't to be trusted."

She blinked at that.

"You?"

"I'm no saint, Meg. I may not lie to you the way Alan did or make promises I don't intend to keep, but don't fall into the trap of believing that I'm better than I am. The one good thing I *can* say for myself is that I never make promises I can't keep to women anymore."

"Not even about this business?"

He gave her a grim smile. "I have high hopes for this business, but there are no guarantees. Mistakes are sometimes made that can't be called back."

Meg was pretty sure that he was thinking of his wife then, but she had no right to ask. She appreciated the gentle warning, however. Maybe he *had* just been trying to tell her that he wouldn't be like Alan, but she had needed a reminder that it would be dangerous to get too close to Etienne. And there was no secret about that. She already knew that he was a man who would only be in her life for a short while. His world and hers would not intersect once he returned to France.

"I should get back to work," she said.

He looked down at her then. "When I made that comment about women and promises, I hope you know that I wasn't implying anything, Meg. I didn't mean that you might be thinking of me romantically. I wouldn't be so arrogant as to presume that."

He ran one hand back through his hair and Meg couldn't help laughing.

"What?"

"You," she said. "Since we met two days ago, you always seem so self-possessed, so in control and calm and cool. Now you're flustered because you're worried I might have thought you were warning me not to fall in love with you."

"I never thought you might be."

Which only made her laugh again. "Etienne, have *you* looked in the mirror lately? Half the women in the office, old and young, are smoothing their hair and re-applying their lipstick when they hear the office door open. I'll bet they're all horribly disappointed when it's me and not you who appears."

"But you're their friend."

"Yes, but I don't have a Y chromosome, broad male shoulders and a French accent. I don't think you need to apologize for warning women away if there's no chance you're going to fall for them. It's only fair to let them know you're not available."

He shook his head. "Yes, but it still feels arrogant to say so."

"Better than letting them think you might be interested."

"Should I wear a sign saying that I'm not available?"

She grinned. "That would be interesting, but I don't

think it's necessary. In an office this size word gets around quickly."

"Ah, the rumor mill. Who starts these rumors, I wonder."

"In this case," she said, with a mock curtsy, "I will."

"Meg Leighton, spreading rumors?"

"Spreading the truth," she corrected. "It's a tough job but hey, someone has to volunteer to do it." And she sighed.

"You are a very admirable woman," he said.

"Ah, more pretty compliments. I love them," she teased. Where had this man been all her life? And where would he be in two months?

Gone. The answer came in a flash. She'd be wise not to forget it.

CHAPTER FIVE

THE next few days went by in a blur of work, work and more work. The entire company had to be inspected, taken apart and put back together, and Etienne marveled at the enthusiasm with which Meg and her team tackled every task. He might be the planner and the one with the experience, but once he had made a decision, Meg led her troops full steam ahead into whatever he asked them to do.

What's more, she was a creative genius, so when he suggested that, besides updating their product, they needed to make the building suggest the appearance of a thriving concern, she drew up some ideas.

Now, here she was beside him, looking a bit uncertain. "Problems?" he asked.

"I… It's the paint for the office." She fidgeted with the poppy-red scarf at her waist. Meg's penchant for color wouldn't quite let her go the monochromatic route, Etienne had noted, and red was her favorite. It was a charming habit.

"There's a problem with…paint?"

She sighed. "I'm sure that you wouldn't find it a problem, but…see, I feel perfectly comfortable handling

whim and let emotion color my decision, I will talk to the police off the record. What happened to Cicely concerns Cicely, the school and the staff."

Athena listened to his no-nonsense message. His adamant announcement about his emotion and whims were like a douse of cold water. She suspected that he would involve the police, on the record. But she was afraid to ask what the punishment would be. His fury over what had happened to Cicely couldn't just evaporate.

She brushed past him with rising irritation.

Her disappointment of his not acknowledging what had transpired between them also irked her. She wasn't stupid about the ramifications. But she felt that it wasn't a mistake.

That kiss had stirred her passion into a heated brew. It had flowed through her system like hot lava.

Being completely ignored didn't sit well with her. She wanted a release for the pent-up feelings that she couldn't dismiss. She wanted more.

"We've got to talk." Collin's hand closed over her wrist, keeping her within inches of him. She rested her palm against his chest, straining to keep her body away from his. His proximity had the potential to make her melt. She didn't want to play games. The rules were too complicated.

"I want to say sorry for last night," he whispered.

"No. Please don't." Athena rested her head gently against his chin. "No regrets. It makes that moment cheap like two adults carrying on without regard."

"I don't want you to be uncomfortable because of my actions."

"Maybe you would feel better if I removed your guilt and laid it squarely at my feet."

Collin squinted; his hand relaxed its grip around her wrist. "How would you do that?"

"I would jump in with both feet." Athena hadn't planned any of this. But adrenaline coursed through her veins. Maybe it clouded her judgment. Maybe the surge to her system nibbled away at her inhibitions.

In this semidarkened spot in the hallway, she was only a few steps from emerging into the bright outdoors. To do so would kill anything on the verge of happening. The alternative would decisively shove her next action into the ever-widening chasm of guilty seduction.

That's what her body craved. One thing, one person, could satisfy her need.

She slid her hand behind his head before tiptoeing to meet his lips. Hell, it might be her last stand. She wasn't going down without a fight.

She kissed his mouth with a possessive fervor that coaxed him until she heard his guttural response. She kept up the frenzy, demonstrating that she had the stamina, power and redemption during a time when so much lay at risk.

She craved the strength of his mouth, firm, masculine, sexy and sensual. She planted kisses against his full lips, intermittently tasting him with the peppered touch of her tongue.

His restraint broke like a dam against a single-minded tide of her attention. He pushed her back against the wall, pinning her hands over her head. He leaned back, staring at her mouth as if he saw something there only for him.

While he kissed her, he pushed his thigh between hers. Athena pushed against his chest, but his hands still pinned hers. She groaned with frustration at not being able to set her hands all over his body.

They warred with each other, their lips and tongues performing guerrilla warfare along each other's cheeks, chin and throat. But when he licked the indentation under her throat, she gasped and pushed off with surprising strength. Warm sizzling feelings spiraling out of control blossomed between her legs, eliciting a moist reaction.

He unbuttoned her shirt, flinging back each side. Without undue effort, he scooped her toward him by the small of her back. The movement raised her chest toward his face. Her breasts anticipated his touch. She wanted to be free of the lace contraption shielding her nipples from his mouth.

He unsnapped the bra behind her back and she slipped it off, not wanting to be bothered with any restriction. He cupped her breasts in his palms, rubbing his thumb against her sensitive nipples. Each swipe made the ache between her legs that much stronger.

"You drive me insane, woman."

Athena heard the agonized wail like a distant call. She'd fallen into a swoon from the hypermadness that had her senses in a whirl.

"I can't do this." This time Collin's declaration sounded urgent, breaking the thin surface.

The crack allowed enough reality to cool the edges of her ardor.

"We can't keep doing this." Collin pulled her shirt closed before turning away for her to redress. "I don't do this. I don't act this way." He held his head in his hands as if his head hurt.

Athena dressed quickly. "I don't have a habit of this, either." Maybe he thought she was a floozy. But far from it, she hadn't dated much after college. Her focus on her finance career and then the switch to teaching took all of her time. Yet she didn't attribute her reaction to Collin as a binge.

"I don't think that I should stick around."

His constant denial for what had transpired irritated her. What happened wasn't ugly and to be ashamed of. She buttoned her blouse and shoved it in her pants.

"I don't think that we should be alone together. We'll try to act like responsible adults. I will observe you at your job, make recommendations. You will help Cicely along and get her back on her feet. If you need anything just let Lorraine know. She's the one responsible for training."

Athena listened and tried not to roll her eyes. How could she be attracted to this man who lived by rules? How hard would he fight his body's response, its needs? The next time, and there would be a next time, he would have to beg her for attention.

She saluted him when he finally stopped talking. He adjusted his clothing, shook his head once more and re-treated to his car.

Collin didn't go home right away. To sit in his living room would invite his memory to recall the sweet temptation he delved into with Athena. The woman would be his downfall.

He needed something to take out his aggression.

the books or the employees or the orders, but as for choosing paint… I'd really, really appreciate your input. I have this teensy little habit of fixating on colors that are overly bright."

She did. He adored that, but for this, she was right. The office needed to have the right look for the brochure they were making.

"All right, let's go buy paint."

Meg shook her head. "Oh, there's no need. I stopped by the store and picked up some color cards yesterday. I narrowed it down, picked out a few and got some samples to try on the wall. I just want you to tell me what you think of the results. I found a corner of the room where I painted a few squares. All you have to do is tell me which square is the right one."

She led him into the main room and over to the spot she had indicated. There were four large colored squares painted on the chalk-white wall. There was a very pale almost invisible blue, a classic colonial-blue, a bold darkish blue and the last, a dazzling electric-blue.

"That last one looked better on the card," Meg explained, clearly embarrassed. "I just… I need to see things, but even I can tell that one won't do. It's a bit shocking, isn't it?"

Just then, a man stepped up to the water cooler not ten feet away. He stared at the squares, pretending to shield his eyes.

"Whoa, Meg, did you do this? Take it easy, will you? You're going to blind me with that bright blue."

Meg smiled self-consciously…and noticed that Etienne had moved to her side.

"What does that man—Jeff?—what job is he involved in?" Etienne asked, his voice low.

"Excuse me?" she said, lowering her voice to match his own.

"What task in particular is he working on?"

"He's... I believe he's working on the payroll statements."

"All right. Good. Ask him when you can expect them on your desk. Say it calmly but firmly," Etienne instructed.

"Is there a reason you need to know? He's right there."

"And you're right here, too." Etienne said. "A woman who wants to establish her place in the business world and wants to know how to do it."

She looked at him for several seconds, then took a visible deep breath and turned with a curt nod despite the concern in her expression. The other man was almost ready to leave the water cooler. "Jeff, excuse me, but could you tell me how far along you are on those payroll statements? I'd like them on my desk sometime today. It's not something I can wait on."

The uncertain woman had been replaced by a cool, confident one. The man did a double take. He looked at Etienne with a question in his eyes, but Etienne ignored him, so the man turned back to Meg.

"Today?"

For a moment Etienne saw Meg hesitate. She didn't want to push the issue.

"I know you can do it," she said softly. "I have faith in your abilities, Jeff."

The man gave her a shaky and grateful smile. "Thank you. And getting them to you today won't be a problem, Meg... I mean, Ms. Leighton," he said.

Her answering smile was glorious and if the man had looked as if he'd been hit with a rock before, now he took on the expression of a man who had been hit by Cupid himself. "Thank you so much, Jeff. Your expertise and promptness is making things run so much more smoothly."

"In an hour, Ms. Leighton," Jeff said. "You'll have them in an hour." He smiled at her again as he moved away.

Etienne waited for him to be gone. Then he turned to Meg.

"Well, *ma chère*, what do you need me for? You're a complete natural," he said. "I only meant for you to start making the switch from being his colleague to being his employer, but you moved him directly from employee to willing slave status."

"He was only being truthful about the bright blue," she said, wrinkling her nose at the vivid color.

"Maybe so, but he has to depend on you now. You outrank him and he needs to know that when he has a problem, you can help. If you don't maintain that employer-employee status, your friends and colleagues will have no one to direct them when I'm gone," he said.

Meg looked at him with those big, bright solemn eyes. Etienne worried that she, who had faced far too much criticism over the years, might be hurt by his comments, but she nodded. "I'll work on that, but I'll probably stumble now and then."

"You have an affinity for the job. You'll do fine."

"You're a good instructor," she said. "But we still have a problem." She looked toward the room.

"Ah, the color. Let's go with the dark blue with ivory trim. When it comes in…we paint."

"Us?" she asked with a smile.

"All of us," he said, indicating the room.

"Oh," she said, and he wondered if she was going to tell him that painting was beneath her dignity or that it wasn't what she'd had in mind when she'd told him she wanted to be a successful businesswoman.

Suddenly Meg grinned and wrinkled her nose in such a cute way that Etienne's heart flipped around a bit. "Don't look at me that way. I happen to love painting," she said. "The chance to slap stuff on a pristine wall with no repercussions? What's not to love?"

And for some reason, Etienne believed her. There was just something irresistible about watching Meg when she was enthused about something.

The painting had gone faster than she had anticipated, Meg thought several days later when most of the employees had gone home and she and Etienne were the only ones left.

"Everything looks good, doesn't it?" she asked, staring around the room. The paint had made such a difference.

"It does. It looks amazing," Etienne agreed and she looked up to see him looking at her.

She suddenly felt self-conscious in her baggy jeans and white T-shirt with a tear at the shoulder. She had lots of paint on her, especially on the part of her shirt right over her left breast, where she had accidentally brushed against the wall. She was a mess, but Etienne... That man could do wonderful things to a black T-shirt and a pair of white painter's pants. Today was the first day she had seen him wearing something other than a white shirt and tie. He was mouthwatering in business attire but the T-shirt revealed tanned muscled biceps that made her want to stare.

She forced herself to look away. "I'm glad we did the painting ourselves," she said, trying to change the subject quickly so that he wouldn't notice her staring.

"It was fun. I love having the chance to relax and just get messy."

"I love watching you get messy," he said suddenly, affection deepening his voice.

Her breath caught in her throat. "I…"

"You're shocked that I said that about you. Frankly, so am I," he said, his voice washing over her. She couldn't turn around. She was too afraid that the naked desire in her eyes would be visible.

"You're right about the satisfaction involved in doing this ourselves," he said. "I could have paid to have someone paint, but it's a task everyone here could take part in. And when I'm gone, I want to leave you in charge, but as I've mentioned, I want the employees to own the company. When people own something, they fight for it. Painting the office was a start to staking their claim. By their own hands they've improved it."

Then Meg couldn't stay turned away from him anymore. "You are going to be missed."

"I'm still here for a number of weeks," he said. "And we're not even close to done yet. Even today…"

"A new lesson for me?" she asked.

"Not quite." He reached out and lifted a long strand of her hair. "You have golden lights in your hair," he said. No one had ever said anything like that to her, especially not with that appreciative tone of voice. Meg swallowed hard. "You also have paint in your hair. I'm taking you to a stylist."

"You're going to cut my hair?" She almost whispered the words. Why did the thought alarm her? She had no reason to be vain about her hair. It was just plain brown hair.

"I wouldn't think of it, unless, of course, that was

what *you* wanted. It's your hair and a very personal part of you, Meg. I'm just suggesting that we shape it and cut out the paint. Would that be all right?"

He was asking her to trust him, though he hadn't said the words. She wanted to say yes. Unlike painting, styling her hair was one of those things she wasn't good at. Her father had disliked any reminders that he had produced a second, unwanted daughter and watching Meg fuss with her hair had always made him snarl. So she hadn't developed the skill. As for trusting Etienne, hadn't trusting people been what got her into so much trouble over the years? She wanted Etienne's help but she also needed to retain some pieces of herself.

"I'd like to talk to the stylist myself," she ventured.

He nodded. "Of course. Do you have a favorite one?"

"I don't have one at all."

"All right. I can take care of that."

In no time at all, they were in a shop where the chairs were more luxurious than her furniture at home. The stylist, Daniel, asked her what she had in mind.

Panic ensued, and Meg sighed. She turned to Etienne. "I have no clue, but…" she maintained. "At least I got to say that much."

Etienne chuckled. "You did. You took charge, and if at any time during this procedure you're alarmed at how it's going we can stop."

"No," Daniel said. "I'm an artist. I don't do things halfway."

"I respect that," Etienne said. "But Meg is a person, and I don't want her to have any regrets."

"She won't."

Etienne gave Meg a look. She knew that she had to be wearing that total panic mode expression.

"Long," Etienne said in a tone that brooked no argument. "Just clean it up, shape it. Take as little off the length as possible."

And just like that, knowing that Etienne wasn't going to let her turn into a disaster zone, Meg relaxed. "About two inches shorter than what it is, I think," she said. "Shoulder length."

"Good," Daniel said. "You'd look good with some layers framing your face. Just a bit for softness. And bangs. Not everyone can carry off bangs, even though most people think they can. You can."

"Daniel thinks I can wear bangs," she said to Etienne. "What do you think about that?" All these compliments might have gone to her head if she wasn't so thoroughly grounded in reality.

"I think Daniel is an artist," Etienne said with a smile. "You know how you feel about painting? Well, I'd say that Daniel feels that way about hair."

She looked up at the tall, bony man who was waiting a bit impatiently. "Sorry for all the discussion and nail biting. It's a life changing issue. But…okay. You're the artist. Give me bangs."

He did, and they were full and bouncy and Meg loved them. The soft tendrils that swept across her cheekbones made her feel feminine. When they left the shop she glanced in the window outside to see her dim and wavy reflection.

"It still looks as good as it did in the shop," Etienne told her.

"Thank you," she said.

"It was all Daniel," Etienne told her.

But it hadn't been. No one else had ever even seemed to care what her hair looked like. Of course, this was just all part of the deal she had struck with Etienne, but he could have simply given her a few tips on how to go on in the business world. Although she had used the word transformation, she hadn't expected to feel so different and free and...aware of herself as a woman.

"Then thank you for taking me to Daniel," she insisted. "You are a great person."

But her comment didn't elicit Etienne's customary charming, dimpled smile. She missed it.

CHAPTER SIX

ETIENNE knew he had to be careful with Meg. She had been so joyful, even grateful after Daniel had turned her already pretty hair beautiful. And she was starting to think that Etienne was better than he was.

That would be disastrous. With his annual anniversary date drawing nearer, dread was starting to creep in now and then. He was far too aware of who and what he was. If Meg saw him as a good guy, and he ended up disappointing her... If her faith in him led to him harming her in any way...

It wasn't going to happen.

For the next week he threw himself into work, trying to map out every angle, to figure out all the ways to make Fieldman's come back to life. He and Meg oversaw the day-to-day operations, the cleanup of the building. He bought new computers, had the outside of the building sandblasted and had the new sign installed.

A photographer came and took photos of the interior, the exterior and of the three sample pieces of furniture Don Handry had managed to complete in record time.

Not trusting himself to spend too much time alone with Meg, Etienne drove himself, but the day came when there was no getting around what came next. He had a feeling Meg was going to…what was the term? Freak out just a little.

After everyone went home, he walked over to the open door of her office and peeked inside. She was bent over her desk, her soft, pretty hair swaying softly. As she worked, she ran those pretty long fingers over the keys of the keyboard gracefully, her eyes intent on the screen. She had no idea that he was there.

Etienne cleared his throat, and she jumped. One hand fluttered at her throat. She was wearing a plain white blouse and a navy skirt today. Very prim, except for the three red bracelets that clanked on her wrists and the red toes of her navy pumps. Meg certainly loved red. And red loved Meg, he couldn't help noticing. It looked good against her pale skin. Which was as far as he was going to allow himself to take that train of thought.

"I'm sorry that I startled you, but I had something I needed to speak to you about," he said.

"Of course," she said, rising as he entered the room.

"I have to apologize to you," he said.

"For what?"

"We have an appointment with some of the smaller local newspapers in—" he looked at his watch "—about forty-five minutes."

Meg's eyes widened. "Etienne, I'm— You know I'm not ready for this." Her voice cracked and then it rose.

"You are. You know every plan we've made, every step we've taken. When I leave here, you'll be the one in charge if you opt to stay. You're the voice. You're the face. You can do this, Meg. I'll be with you," he said. "Every step of the way."

"I don't know enough to do this."

"You know you do. Already, you're overseeing a lot of the operations."

"But that's different. People here are people I know. Some of them were here when I got here. They don't mind when I trip with these new shoes and end up slamming into a desk. They just smile and go on. And when I laugh too loud or wear colors that clash, they don't mind. It doesn't matter. They don't write it in a newspaper so everyone can read about it with their morning coffee."

Etienne stepped closer. He took her hands in his own. "Meg, look at me."

She did, and he was shocked to see that her eyes were glistening.

"You're— Meg, you're… Tears? I— Dammit, I didn't tell you ahead of time because I didn't want you to make yourself sick worrying. Now I've frightened you so much that you're going to cry." If ever a man wanted to kick himself, it was him right now, Etienne thought. "Meg… I'm… Forgive me, but…"

"No. I am *not* going to cry just because I'm a little scared," she said, shaking her head vigorously. "It's embarrassing and silly and unacceptable and juvenile and…I just won't. I never do. Not for years."

His heart split right there and then. She hadn't cried for years and he was the jerk who had brought her to the verge. But he could see that she was going to be as good as her word. She was fighting her fear with every ounce of strength she possessed.

"Ah, Meg, I'm so sorry," he said, pulling her to him, his arms going around her. "I thought that I could easily convince you of the truth, that you'll be just fine. I won't let you fall. I won't sacrifice you."

He wanted to look into her pretty brown eyes so that she could see that he meant every word. But Meg had hidden her face against his chest. She was probably embarrassed.

"Fine independent businesswoman I'm turning out to be. I ask for your help and then at the first hint of anything stressful, I'm running away and squawking. Etienne, I'm truly ashamed for carrying on this way," she said, confirming his assumptions. "I should know better. It's just… I'm not very good yet at being a public person with strangers. I haven't learned enough yet."

"You're very good with *me*."

"You're different."

"How?"

"You're…you."

He smiled as the muffled word echoed through his skin against his heart. He started to tighten his hold. She felt good against him, but suddenly she pulled back and looked directly up at him, straight into his eyes, her caramel eyes glistening, although no tears had fallen.

"I really am sorry for being such an idiot," she said. "I… The only very bad explanation I can give is that…my parents had me when they were older. They had a grown daughter by then and they didn't want another. In fact, they had been planning to divorce, but then I came along and they felt they had to stay married. My father might have been okay with me if I had been a son, my mother might have been okay if I had been pretty like Ann, but I wasn't either of those things. I was…not what they had signed on for, and then, one of those rare days when my mother was happy, she swung me in a circle, playing, but I was too big and we fell. I cut my cheek. After that, she not only wished I was pretty like Ann, she wished she could wipe away the scar she felt she had caused. To her I was a reminder of the mistakes she and my father had made. After that, they more or less ignored me.

"I read a lot, camped out in front of the television and gained weight. My reticence, my awkwardness and my height made me stand out at school, and not in a good way, either. So, I kept to myself and I never learned how to interact with people the way most women do. Except for here where Mary protected me."

"Meg, don't criticize yourself," Etienne said, stroking her hair.

She shook her head. "I didn't tell you this so that you would feel sorry for me."

"I don't. You're unique and I mean that in the best way."

"It's just… I'm sorry that I made such a fuss. It's hard for me to be a public person. It's what I want to be able to do. It's why I asked you to help me, and all right, I'm past my little fit. I'll be better in a few minutes."

Etienne saw red. He absolutely shouldn't have done this without telling her. What's more, he should have known all this about her background. Many people, maybe even most suffered from stage fright, but Meg had been forced to apologize for her appearance and for her very existence to the two people who should have pledged themselves to nurture and love her. And here he had gone and made things difficult for her and she was actually trying to apologize to him!

He gazed down into her eyes, those earnest, lovely eyes. Her lips were parted and he just knew she was going to try to reassure him some more and tell him that she would be fine, that he was not to worry that he had ambushed her.

It was too much. Etienne gave a small tug and pulled her deeper into his arms. He took her mouth with his own and swallowed her soft gasp of surprise.

Her body molded to his and for several seconds she was still as he tasted her, breathed her in and worshipped her lips. She was soft and very sweet and…

Meg shifted against him. She looped her arms around his neck and tilted her head. Her lips slid beneath his own, and flame shot through him.

A small moan escaped her, driving him insane to have more of her. He deepened the kiss, took more of her. He plunged his hands into those soft curls to hold her still.

But she wouldn't be still. Her body slid over his as she returned his kiss, and the heat climbed higher within him.

He wanted her. All of her. Right here. In this room. Right now. He wanted her for hours. For days. And to hell if anyone returned to the office who would wonder what was going on, who would remember how she had been taken advantage of by a man before…

Etienne groaned and stilled.

Meg froze.

"I'm sorry," he said, as they disentangled themselves.

"Please don't say that."

"I have to."

"No. Don't apologize. If you have to be sorry, don't tell me so."

And Etienne realized just what she meant. She had almost moved away completely, but he gently tried to pull her back.

Meg resisted.

"If you think I meant that I was sorry for wanting you, then you're very wrong." Even though he *was* sorry for that. Wanting her complicated things when he wasn't going to stay.

"It's all right."

"No. It isn't. I'm not Alan, Meg."

How did the Americans say it? Bingo. Her eyes came to rest on him, and he saw the truth.

"When you and I touch, there's nothing pretend about it for me," he told her. "I desire you, very much. If I'm sorry, it's not because the kiss was a lie but because it wasn't. You and I…touching or…doing more… I can't stay, Meg. I won't lie to you about that. That's why I'm sorry. I shouldn't start something I can't follow through on."

She smiled then. Actually smiled when his body was screaming with the need to pull her to him. And then a sad little look came on her face. "All that moving around you do… I… It's none of my business, I have no right to even ask why, but…"

"Her name was Louisa," he said. "I'd known her forever. She was shy but not with me. Our families knew each other and from the day Louisa and I were born, our parents joked about how Louisa and I would marry. Only when my father died, it wasn't a joke anymore. I was the only remaining Gavard male, and my mother pinned all her hopes on me. I inherited the Gavard estate and all the responsibilities and commitments and history that that entailed. I was expected to do the right thing, marry the right woman, have the right child. So, I did all those things. Or I attempted to.

"I hated it, but it was my duty and my mother grew hysterical at the thought that I might fail the family name. So, I married Louisa and found out that she loved me. And also found out that I could break her heart because I was gone all the time on business. Fragile and afraid of my mother's intimidating ways, she stayed alone or in the Paris penthouse, and she was bitterly unhappy when I was gone."

Meg bit her lip. Her eyes were dark with concern. "Etienne, I shouldn't have pried. You don't have to tell me this."

"Maybe I need for you to know. I came here to save Fieldman's, but I don't ever want you to think that I'm better than I am. Do you understand?"

Slowly she nodded. "You want me to think that you're worse than you are."

If the next part wasn't so awful, he might have smiled. Instead he shook his head. "I used Louisa to achieve my goals. Marry a woman of good family? Check. I did that. Beget an heir?"

He paused. "She didn't even want children at first, but she felt that if she had the Gavard heir, I would stay home. And I wanted her to have it. But even when she was pregnant, even once she had explained why she agreed to get pregnant, I didn't slow down my business trips. I wasn't even there when the stress of pregnancy and an undetected congenital heart defect precipitated a heart attack that took her life and the life of our son." Anger at his inability to go back and change things, to take back all his mistakes, left him suddenly speechless.

Meg touched his hand. "How could you have known?" she said softly. "I know you would have prevented their deaths if there was any way you could have, Etienne."

But he couldn't respond. No matter the situation, no matter how much he wished he could reverse time and change the results of that day, he couldn't. He had failed Louisa long before the day of her death. He had broken her heart. And when, after Louisa's death, he'd told his mother that he was abdicating his place as the head of the family, dropping control of the family firm except for this small part he had started himself, and that he would not even consider ever starting another family, he'd broken her heart and failed her, too. Because after that, no matter how many times he apologized for his careless, thoughtless words, she felt responsible for pushing him into grief and she died feeling that way.

The truth was that he was hell on women. He disappointed and hurt them without trying. But, he promised himself, not this time. Please not this time.

He looked at Meg. She looked so sad, so chagrined. "I opened up old wounds by being nosy and speaking out of turn the way I always do. I— I'm so sorry I intruded."

Etienne shook his head. "No. It needed to be out in the open so that you understand completely, Meg. I've had reason in my life to regret how I've handled my associations with women, but that's not going to happen this time. I won't give you false promises of any kind," he told her, "but I won't disappoint you by failing to help you, either. Beyond business I have no right to get involved with anyone and you have the right to know that. Because when I go, I'm going to miss you. But I'm still going to have to go. I never stay. I can't."

She didn't blink, didn't flinch. Finally she took a step closer rather than a step farther away. "Then, if the clock is ticking, I'd better start learning how to be a totally independent woman and head of this company quickly, hadn't I? I'd better learn all the lessons you're willing to help me with, Etienne. I don't want you to have regrets. Instead I want to be a testament to your training, a worthy protégée. I'm going to do it. With your help, I'm going to go meet those newspaper people right now and be all that you intend for me to be."

She stood before him, tall and elegant and full of confidence, and he had never been so proud of her. But he had also never been so sad to think about the future. Never getting to see her again when his time here was up was going to be…difficult.

But it would happen, nonetheless. He couldn't even think about staying and taking the risk of seeing Meg hurt or growing to hate him.

CHAPTER SEVEN

THE room where the meeting was taking place was large with a conference table and cushy, big blue chairs. Ten of the twelve chairs were taken up by reporters, mostly female, all in black suits, and when Meg and Etienne walked in, Meg wanted to turn around and walk right back out again.

But she didn't. She didn't even look at Etienne even though she knew that if she did, he would be staring back at her, offering strength and encouragement. She wondered what he'd think if she told him that she was the girl who got poor grades on her oral presentations in school because she was so self-conscious that she stammered and forgot what she needed to say.

It didn't matter. She wasn't going to tell him. And she was going to do this right. Because Etienne was carrying too much guilt on his shoulders. She didn't want to be another weight, another woman he'd end up regretting. Besides, she might be the face of Fieldman's, but he was the actual owner, the one taking the biggest risk, and she wasn't going to fail him if she could help it. She prayed that she could come off looking reasonably competent. Or at least not incompetent.

Besides, hadn't she wanted to forge a place for herself in the world, to be a woman to be reckoned with, to become so self-sufficient that she didn't need to depend on a man for anything? Well, here was her chance. She needed to take it and she had to remember that wanting a man like Etienne would be self-destructive, a one-way ticket to doom and gloom and certain heartbreak. Anyone with any intelligence could see that.

Meg circled around to the open side of the table, facing the reporters. She tried to recall all the things she and Etienne had spoken about on the way over here, all his coaching, all the statistics and talking points she was supposed to spout, but the only thing she could really remember was his admonition to "be yourself. Just be Meg."

Meg looked at the group gathered there. She opened her mouth, uncertain of what she intended to say. It was school report day all over again, but then she looked at Etienne. His silver-blue eyes held no hint of concern. He was smiling at her. He believed in her.

"I have the most wonderful job in the world," Meg began, which was nothing like what she and Etienne had decided on. "Because I've been very lucky and because I've been blessed to be able to work with wonderful people.

"I got my start at Fieldman's when I was sixteen. I left a year ago and then was rehired a few weeks ago by Mr. Gavard," she said, nodding toward Etienne. "We're…partners and with the help of the other employees of Fieldman's we intend to not only reenergize the company, but to make it the kind of place people will compete to work for. It's going to be a furniture friendly, consumer friendly, environmentally friendly and employee friendly company. We've already started. Let me show you."

She pulled out her portfolio of the new product line and some of the ideas she and Etienne had drawn up to make Fieldman's, small though it was, stand out from the crowd.

"Every drop of paint we use, every piece of technology we buy will be planet friendly. Our furniture is handmade out of materials that are certified chemical free for those people who have medical concerns."

"Isn't that expensive?"

"It is. That's why we're grateful that Mr. Gavard has taken over the company, although…he intends to eventually sell most of his shares to the employees."

"Mr. Gavard," one reporter said. "What do you say to all this?" The woman was eyeing Etienne as if he were a piece of man-size chocolate she wanted to bite into.

"This is not my show," he said. "I refer all questions to Ms. Leighton."

"Your…partner," the woman said. Then she turned suddenly to Meg.

"Is he really just your partner?"

Meg blinked. How to react? How not to overreact? Instructions flew through her head. Reactions begged to be spoken. She ignored them.

Then she smiled. "Ms. Banner," she said, reading the woman's badge. "Look at me. I'm a…decent-looking woman. I have my attributes, I rather like this new hairdo I have, don't you? But, I ask you…do I seriously look anything at all like the kind of woman Mr. Gavard would be entangled with? The man is absolutely gorgeous and he's got those great dimples and… Well, of course I like looking at him, but most of you here would make much more likely dating material for Mr. Gavard should he be looking for a date."

Every woman in the room turned to look at Etienne. Meg smiled and waved.

"He has dimples?" one woman asked.

"Oh, yeah," Meg said. "And when he doesn't believe something, he can do this great, sexy thing with his eyebrow. Show them the sexy eyebrow thing, Etienne."

He crossed his arms. "I think this press conference was supposed to be about Fieldman's, wasn't it, *partner*?"

"Oh, now he's going to get all professorial on us and give us a lecture. I probably won't be able to even drag him out to another one of these if you write something about him and not the furniture," Meg confided.

"Nice manipulative move, Ms. Leighton," one reporter said.

"Yes, and we'll bite," another one answered. "Usually we're just attending boring meetings. You bring Mr. Gavard back for us to drool over and we'll be right there."

"See if you can get him to take his shirt off next time," one woman teased.

"You just make sure you write something nice about Fieldman's and I might talk him into rolling up his shirt-sleeves," Meg promised.

The women laughed. Even the two men in the crowd looked amused. "You're totally cute," one said to Meg.

Meg's mouth fell open. "Well…thank you," she said.

"And I think your ideas for Fieldman's and your products are going to stir up a lot of attention at the local trade shows."

"Will you say that in your article?"

"Absolutely. It's what I do."

Meg smiled and nodded and fielded another question. When the meeting finally ended and the room had emptied, Etienne walked toward her. "That was the most unconventional press conference I've ever attended," he said.

Meg played with the buttons on her suit. "You've attended a lot, haven't you?"

"Thousands." He moved forward two feet.

"And none like this? Hmm."

"'Hmm' is right. I didn't see any statistics."

"I kind of forgot about those in the heat of the moment." He took another step closer.

"No schedules."

"Forgot that, too."

"And no mention of your impending trip to Paris and the international arm of the company."

"I'm sure I'll remember to talk about that next time."

"And…what was that about my sexy dimples and how you were going to talk me into rolling my shirt-sleeves up?"

"But I totally saved you from having to take your shirt off. I didn't think you'd want to do that, even though it would've livened things up a bit."

And he took the last step toward her, slid his hands up her arms, walked her back three steps to the wall and gently pinned her against the wall.

He kissed her. Totally. Thoroughly. Completely. A kiss that was wet, hot and made her knees forget their job of holding her up.

She slid.

He caught her.

And kissed her again.

"This was not a press conference," he said. "This

was major torture for me. I can't take having you look at me like you want to climb into bed with me, especially if you're doing it merely for the sake of theater. Now kiss me, Meg."

She did.

He smiled and did that amazing Etienne dimple move. "You were marvelous," he said. "Don't do it again."

"Don't kiss you?" she asked, teasing him even though her heart was beating wildly, her blood was rushing around her body and her entire being was hot and crazy and on fire for one more kiss, one more touch.

"Don't tease me while other people look on. Seriously. I can't take it, Meg. I was in danger of walking over there and pulling you down on the table right in front of everyone. That just wouldn't be right."

"No," she agreed. "Because then everyone would want some of that."

"You make me crazy," he told her.

"You make me crazier, but, Etienne?" Reality was returning. Her lips were burning. Reality was intruding and she was afraid. Really afraid. She hadn't even hesitated or protested or thought while he was kissing her. This man could break her, so easily.

"I know," he said, brushing her cheek with his thumb. "We can't do this, and I have no right to blame you, Meg. You were just working the crowd. You really were spectacular. They liked you, all of them. Especially the men."

He frowned.

"They were just being nice."

"No. You have what it takes to win people over. You just didn't know it before."

Because she'd just never had someone like Etienne telling her things like this before.

"You're going to be fine. You're going to be great. You're going to make it," he told her.

And she knew that he was thinking about all the things that would happen after he was gone. He had said that there were no guarantees in life, but she could tell that there was one. One day Etienne would board a plane. And then it would be just her. Without him. Forever.

She had to stop wanting him. Right now. The wisest thing to do would be to keep her distance from him.

But that just wasn't going to happen. At least not yet.

CHAPTER EIGHT

EVER since Meg had fallen into Etienne's arms like a ripe plum, she had been reminding herself that while she might be enjoying herself now, the time would come when it would just be her and Lightning and the occasional foster cats from the shelter. If she was very lucky, she might find some way to have the baby she wanted, but even then, she would be a single adult. It would be a total mistake to start thinking that having Etienne around could continue for more than a few weeks.

If she did, she was going to die a thousand emotional deaths. And that just couldn't happen. She needed to channel her fantasies into more productive avenues. No more waking up at three in the morning, dreaming of Etienne in her bed, his lips nuzzled against her neck.

Her dreams had gotten steadily more dangerous. Because of that, she did her best to foster normalcy at work, to plan for her future as a solo adult. So, she read the books Etienne gave her on management techniques. She signed up for some business classes for the fall at a local college. She watched her employees and concentrated on learning their work habits and tending to their needs not only as a friend but as a manager. And she tried not to notice Etienne, who seemed to be driving himself just as hard as she was.

He had been meeting with distributors, meeting with buyers, meeting with everyone but her, she couldn't help noticing. Not that she blamed him. That press conference had been totally outrageous, and possibly embarrassing to Etienne, even if it had spawned a lot of other meetings and a couple of great articles about the company.

Besides, she knew why Etienne was driving himself so hard. There was another reason. When she had pried into his personal life that day, he hadn't mentioned the date of his wife's death, but Meg knew it just the same. There had been rumors in those online articles she'd read about him that last year Etienne had closed himself up in a hotel room and not come out for two weeks. The date was approaching fast. He was obviously trying to work hard, either to punish himself or to forget. Either avenue wasn't healthy.

That just wasn't acceptable. Somehow she needed to be a better friend and partner.

Meg put down the papers she had been looking at and wandered out to find Etienne. She found him with Andy, a computer specialist who moonlighted as a graphic artist. Both men looked up when she came near.

"Look at this, Meg," Etienne said. "This is a mock-up of some ads I thought we might run locally. What do you think?"

She thought that no one other than Mary would have ever asked her that kind of question in the past, but both men looked at her as if expecting her to make an intelligent contribution to the conversation. Warmth swirled through Meg.

"I think the ad and the graphics project have exactly the kind of new look we want for Fieldman's." She hesitated.

"But…" Etienne coached.

Meg looked at Andy.

"Give it to me, boss," he said. "Don't hold back."

"The font just seems a bit too…"

"I knew it," Andy said. "It's too cartoonish. I should have known."

Automatically Meg placed her hand on his shoulder. "No, the whole thing looks great, very visually appealing, and I think in other instances we might use this particular font. Maybe down the line once we've started winning people over. For now, do you have something…I don't know. Bold but still classic? Slightly edgier but not so much so that people will notice the font before the furniture?"

"Yes, that's the problem, isn't it?" he said. "I think… Yes, I've got just the thing. I'll change this and get it back to you asap. And, Ms. Leighton?"

She blinked. She still wasn't used to people calling her Ms. Leighton.

"Good eye," the man said. "Mr. Gavard and I knew that something was off just a bit, but we hadn't decided what." And he went back to his work as if nothing out of the ordinary had happened.

For Meg, however, it was an amazing moment.

"I know it's nothing," she told Etienne, "but I didn't really feel as if I was helping all that much until this moment. It felt as if I was playing at the job."

"You're joking, right? You've been running rings around all of us, Meg."

"Not you."

"Even me. You have a seemingly endless abundance of energy." And then he smiled. There were those intriguing sexy dimples again. Her breathing kicked in. She concentrated on taking slow, deep breaths so that he wouldn't see how he affected her.

"I just…when I'm worried, I tend to move faster, talk faster, do everything faster," she admitted.

"We're doing as much as we can. I don't want you to make yourself sick," he said.

"And I don't want you to make yourself sick, either." She raised her chin.

Etienne considered that. "I feel fine."

"You're driving yourself."

"Bad habit," he admitted.

"I don't think it's a good idea."

"Don't you, Meg?" he asked, and his words sounded like a caress. "Why not?"

"Because." She crossed her arms.

He grinned. "Good reason."

"I'm working on the reason. No, I know what the reason is, but you might think it's silly."

"There's nothing wrong with silly. Sometimes."

She considered that. "It's just…you've been in Chicago for weeks. Have you actually seen any of the city? That is, I know that you know a lot about it, but while you've been here you haven't had time to do anything except take care of Fieldman's and me."

"Ah, you're worrying. Don't worry, Meg. I like taking care of you."

Those words, that deep voice, the way he was looking at her… For a second, Meg wanted to purr like Lightning, to lean in to him. But this wasn't about her giving in to her foolish desires.

"Well…" she said. "That's…that's nice, but now I think it's time that I took care of you."

He raised that brow.

"Don't do that."

"Don't do what?"

"You know. That thing you do with your eyebrow. You're trying to distract me."

He looked mildly amused. "I didn't know it distracted you."

She gave him a "you've got to be kidding" look, but she had made the comment about his eyebrow without thinking and now her thoughts were catching up to her words…as usual. It was probably better not to pursue this topic any further. She didn't want to have to admit how susceptible to him she was.

"All this time you've been the one guiding me. I think…I *want* to be the one to do the guiding this time. Will you have some free time after work?"

"For…?"

"Sightseeing. Playtime. You actually taking a breather from work and getting out into the city for something other than baby-sitting all of us. Me, being the guide for a change."

"You're going to take me out, Meg?"

Okay, she was blushing. She knew she was. Why had she ever thought that she wasn't a blusher? Or, more to the point, why did she only seem to react this way with Etienne? She didn't want to know.

"Is there something wrong with a friend taking a friend out to see the town?" she asked, tilting her chin high.

He grinned. "Not a thing, and yes, I'd be delighted to have you as my tour guide."

They smiled at each other. The phone rang and Meg started to leave. Behind her, Etienne picked up the phone.

"I'm afraid that won't be possible. When you sold the business to me, I made it clear that you were selling everything."

Meg stopped in her tracks as Etienne's voice broke the silence.

"You know that you have absolutely no claim to the Fieldman's name," he said. "And I'm not interested in allowing you to buy back in to the company in any way. Your association with the company and with everyone in it has ended. Don't approach me or anyone here again. Don't call."

Meg's heart started to pound. Hard. She turned back toward Etienne. Her eyes must look huge. She probably even looked a little scared, but she couldn't help it. And she couldn't help noticing that while Etienne's voice had been as cool as ice, his jaw was tight and his hands were curled into fists.

"Has he called you before?" Her voice came out much too softly.

"Once. I barely managed not to ask him to meet me in a dark alley. After the way he treated you, it was what I wanted to do, and it would have made me feel a hell of a lot better to hit him. But getting into a physical altercation with Alan would only hurt you. He's the kind who likes to bring very public lawsuits. But, Meg…"

She waited.

"He can't hurt you. Or anyone here. I've made sure of that. I have an airtight contract. He has no legal recourse. Still, if he ever calls here or approaches you in any way, I want you to call me. I don't think he'd be that stupid, but still… As much faith as I have in your abilities, I don't want you to have to be the one to deal with him."

Her heart stopped pounding. It melted. She barely managed a nod. "Thank you," she said.

Etienne shook his head and gave her a crooked smile. "It's just the way business goes," he said, even though she knew that wasn't true. "Now, weren't we on the verge of going out to have fun?"

"I think I might have promised you something like that."

That was how, just a few hours later, Meg found herself standing under The Bean in Millennium Park.

"It's an odd nickname for something with a name as beautiful as Cloud Gate," Etienne conceded of the highly reflective steel sculpture that did bear a striking resemblance to a bean. "But it's a very beautiful and imposing structure. Look at us, Meg. Look what all that work is doing to our bodies," he teased, as they stared at their distorted images in the sculpture.

She bopped him on the arm. "Etienne, you promised to transform me into a gorgeous woman, not this hideous creature I see here. What have you done to me, you evil man?" she teased.

A group of teenage tourists standing nearby gave the two of them a strange look, and Etienne held out his hands in mock surrender. "She's been working much too hard," he told them, and Meg couldn't help laughing. "Her mind is going."

"Maybe she's a little crazy, but your woman has some fine legs," a boy in the group said.

Etienne chuckled. "I couldn't agree with you more," he said.

"They think we're strange," Meg told him as the two of them moved on through the park.

"And involved," Etienne pointed out.

Instantly Meg sobered. She didn't want him to think that she was growing too attached to him. She didn't want to grow too attached to him. "Well, at least *we* know that we're just business partners."

"And friends," he reminded her.

"Yes. And this friend still has more to show you." It was Thursday and there would be a concert at the Pritzker Pavilion later, but it hadn't started yet, so they walked over to the Crown Fountain, two huge structures connected by a reflecting pool and projecting the ever-changing images of over one thousand Chicago residents. "The kids love it when an image opens its mouth and water flows out. It's pretty cool. Come on." And without another word, Meg took off her shoes, held them in one hand and walked out into the reflecting pool.

Etienne shook his head and followed suit. "When you told me you were going to take me sightseeing, I was picturing something more dignified."

"Museums?"

"Maybe."

"Theater?"

"Of course."

"No dancing in the fountain?"

"Not a chance. That's not sightseeing."

"What is it?"

He laughed. "It's just plain fun, Meg. This was just what I needed. This letting loose."

The two of them joined in with the kids and a few other adults. Etienne took Meg's hand and led her into a romping polka, their feet kicking up water. "It's the only dance I do well," she explained. "It's wild and fast and I can lead and no one seems to notice."

A few minutes later, somewhere in the distance, the concert started up, the majestic and imposing strains of "Respighi's Pines of Rome" echoing throughout the park. The music was beautiful, but Meg's eyelids were beginning to droop.

Etienne led her out of the fountain, made her sit on a bench and reached out for her foot.

"What are you doing?" she asked, instantly awake.

"I'm putting your shoes on."

"I can do that."

"Too late. I already did," he said, deftly cupping her foot in his palm and sliding her shoe on. There was something so intimate about the gesture that Meg felt a tingling running from the sole of her foot all the way up through her body. And then he did it again, with the other shoe.

All traces of tiredness had fled by now.

"Come on, Meg," he said as he put his own shoes back on. "I'm taking you home."

"There were more things I wanted to show you," she said. "Navy Pier. The giant Ferris wheel. The cruises on the lake."

"Another day," he said. "You're tired."

But somehow she knew that there wouldn't be another day. She had started attending functions, talking up the company. Orders were starting to trickle in. The wheels of Fieldman's were picking up speed, and soon she and Etienne would be headed to Paris for one last push at an entirely different set of potential customers. And once the expo in Paris was over…Etienne was over, too.

"Another day," she agreed.

When she opened her apartment door, the phone was ringing. "Go ahead," Etienne said and she moved to answer it. When she returned he was standing in the middle of her apartment. Lightning was flirting with him shamelessly, standing on the couch next to him and rubbing up against him.

"I thought you had *a* cat," he said.

"I do."

"No. I can hear another meow from somewhere." He gestured with his head.

Meg shrugged. "The other cats are Pride and Prejudice." She nodded toward the other room. "They were supposed to simply be foster cats, but they're a pair and difficult to place. They're shy. Eventually, they'll come out." She went about the business of putting food out, talking soothingly to each cat as she fed them.

"And all three cats get along?" Etienne asked.

"They're my family. Family members do not fight other family members. If I can prevent it," she added.

Etienne chuckled. "Are there others?"

"For today, this is it. But it's an unpredictable family and is subject to unexpected growth at any time. The local shelter contacts me now and then when they need help saving an animal and they think I can be of use."

"And you once said that you wanted a child."

Despite the fact that it was Etienne himself who had dropped this conversational nugget in, the room felt as if the temperature had changed. Etienne had been playing along with Lightning and rubbing her head as she purred and leaned against him shamelessly. Now he stopped, his fingers stilling.

"You told me that you were unlikely to get married. How do you plan to get one? A child, I mean."

She looked directly into his eyes. "I don't know yet. I needed to have a stable position before I tried adopting…or maybe I'll go to a sperm bank."

"So…there won't be a father?"

"No. No father."

Because men had not treated her well, he was sure. In the silence that followed her announcement, the slow burn of anger slid through Etienne.

He still hadn't replied to her comment, and Meg picked up the small ginger colored cat that had wandered into the room, nuzzled it and began to pet the animal. "I'll be a good mother," she said, as if promising herself and him that. "I'll care."

"I have no doubt of that."

"You don't approve."

"It's not that at all. It isn't my business to approve or disapprove. I just… You should have help." Etienne studied her attention to the cat. He watched as her fingers threaded through the little cat's fur and then as the third cat, a small ball of black fur, demanded his turn.

"I'll manage," she said. And she could just as easily have added, I always do. But she didn't say those words.

"I suspect you'll do better than manage," he told her. He glanced at the cats. "Pride and Prejudice?" he asked as she put the little black cat down and soothingly spoke to the pair as they went on their way.

She shrugged. "It's my favorite book."

"I see. So, of course you'd name two cats after it just as you'd name a cat who never jumps and barely even blinks Lightning."

"Of course. I have a unique naming system. It's called the impulse system," she said with a small smile, but when she had bent over to release the cat, her hair had snagged on her lips. Without thought, Etienne stepped forward and brushed it away. His fingertips touched her mouth.

His gaze settled there.

He touched her again and lowered his head.

Their lips had barely met, he'd hardly gotten a taste of her, when he heard an enquiring purr and looked down to see Lightning gazing at them like a mother standing guard over her daughter.

"You have a bodyguard."

"No. She likes you."

Etienne had some crazy urge to ask Meg if she liked him, too. He wanted to know how much she liked him.

And that was unacceptable. A man didn't tell a woman he was leaving one day and the next day demand that she pledge her love and loyalty. Hadn't he already destroyed one woman in a relationship where she did all the giving?

"Even if she likes me, I have the feeling that Lightning would protect you if she felt I was up to no good." And kissing Meg couldn't be good even if it felt right.

"Were you up to no good?" Meg asked suddenly.

He leaned in and stole one quick kiss. "Yes. I like kissing you too much. And…I want to do more than kiss you. You make me want more. So, I should thank Lightning for breaking in. And I should go before I do something we'll both end up regretting. Besides, you need rest, and we have a lot to do tomorrow. Lessons," he warned.

"What kind of lessons?"

"Meg lessons. Food and wine. Table settings. Just mundane stuff, in case you ever get asked to one of those boring business dinners. And you will."

"That won't be mundane for me. I don't handle alcohol well at all."

"Well, then, this should be fun."

Then he was gone.

CHAPTER NINE

ETIENNE was not a happy man. It had nothing to do with the fact that during the previous day's lessons he had discovered that Meg and wine were not a pair and that she tended to fall asleep after a single glass. There was something rather endearing about watching her struggle not to yawn and then finally succumb, her head falling softly forward and then jerking up as she attempted to keep herself awake.

Now that he knew her weakness, he could head off trouble easily. She could simply drink water and forget the wine. But drinking wine wasn't the problem.

The problem was this matter of Meg and her family and her family-to-be, something that had been bothering him ever since the other day in her apartment. It was clear as anything that she was a nurturing woman. Just watching her interact with and talk about her cats, that was obvious. Just thinking about the fact that she had been so concerned about his welfare that she had insisted on taking him out for some playtime, or the fact that she had even agreed to come back to Fieldman's, he knew that she was a woman who cared about the welfare of others.

But it was also obvious to him that she had had some pretty brutal parents if they hadn't been able to see what a treasure that she was. And then there had been that complete imbecile Alan who had not recognized Meg for the talented gift of a woman she was. She'd spent too much time trying to please people who couldn't be pleased, but…her cats weren't judgmental. A good scratch behind the ears, a little food and shelter and a woman had a friend for life, one who wouldn't turn on her.

And now she was planning on raising a baby alone.

That wasn't right. Not that she didn't have the talent or the ability or enough love to go around. It was just…she shouldn't always have to be shouldering everything alone.

It burned him. And yet he could do nothing about it. He was, after all, no better than any of the others. He would spend time with her, accept her aid, enjoy her talent and her company and her warmhearted, friendly teasing ways. He had even several times broken his rule of maintaining his distance and she had ended up in his arms. He liked having her in his arms…too much. He wanted to have her in his bed…for hours. But that, all of it, was wrong, because in the end, he would leave her as everyone else had.

So why was he so angry at her parents and Alan? He had no right to be angry on her behalf if he was going to act no better than anyone else had. And maybe that was why he was so upset. Because he had no right. And he never would have.

The phone on his desk rang. When he picked it up, it was the receptionist, Dora, telling him that there was a woman to see him. A woman named Paula Avery. She said the name as if he should know who it was, and it did sound slightly familiar but not enough for him to figure out who the woman was.

And when Paula Avery walked into his office, he still didn't have a clue. It was only after she began talking, her voice fast and nervous as she kept looking over her shoulder, that Etienne began to understand.

He held up both hands. "What you're telling me is that you've worked here before."

"Yes. Recently."

"Who hired you?"

"Alan Fieldman did," she said.

Etienne automatically frowned. He couldn't seem to help it. It was difficult not to hold that against the woman even though it wasn't fair at all. "What was your position?" he continued, trying to soften his tone and set aside his prejudice.

"I was the office manager." And that was when Etienne's resolve flew out the window. He looked down at her application and saw that she had been hired not long before Meg left the company and that she had worked almost up until the time that Alan left. This was the woman Alan had hired instead of promoting Meg.

Anger as hot as a flame rolled over him, but he fought it. Meg had been a total hit with the reporters from the local newspapers and television and radio shows, and she was developing a bit of a fan club. Owning a Fieldman's piece of furniture was becoming trendy. Everyone wanted to be like Meg. It was good for her to finally have some true adulation. She deserved so much more, and he didn't want her associated with anything negative. Following through on his inclination to yell at this woman would only harm Meg. Etienne fought for calm, for a sense of quiet purpose. Years of training kicked in, thank goodness, and he was able to modulate his voice. "I'm sorry, but I'm afraid we don't have anything here for you, Ms. Avery," he said.

"Are you sure? Please. I don't expect anything like the position I held before. But after Alan fired me, I couldn't find work. I... I have children," she said, just as Meg poked her head around the door.

Amazingly the look on Meg's face wasn't as shocked as Etienne would have expected. She was staring at Paula Avery intently and moving closer. He realized that the woman's voice would have carried out into the hallway and that Meg might have recognized it.

"You're applying for a job," she said to the woman.

The woman turned as white as schoolroom paste. "I— I guess I didn't think. That is, I just thought...with Alan gone... I'm sorry. I'll go. Right now."

Her hands shook, her shoulders slumped and she rose to leave.

"Paula, stop. I heard you before," Meg said gently. "You need work."

The woman looked at Meg with suspicion and fear, and her eyes were dark and haunted. "I've tried other places, but my record isn't too great. Alan wouldn't give me a reference. He blamed me for the fact that the company wasn't doing well."

"Why here?" Etienne said suddenly. "Why would you return to a company where you got fired?"

As if he'd just realized what he'd said, as if he'd forgotten that he had begged Meg to do the very same thing, he looked up and his gaze locked with Meg's. Was she all right? She looked tired and sad, but there was a softness about her, a sense of resignation and...acceptance. She didn't look as tense as he might have expected.

"I know it sounds crazy, but…you were hiring. I heard that and…I need to make a living somehow. I'm willing to take whatever you can offer me. Whatever you're willing to give me to do."

Etienne knew as well as he knew anything that Meg's soft heart was going to lead her to offer this woman a job. What he wasn't prepared for what Meg suggested next. "We're acting as a distributor right now for a couple of companies who design for us, but we'd also like to start an experimental in-house line. If I remember correctly you had a background in design. There might be room for an entry level position on the design team if you're interested," Meg said.

The woman murmured a quiet yes. She looked as if she wanted to drop to the ground and hug Meg's legs. "You should hate me," the woman said, clearly confused.

Meg sighed. "You weren't the one who fired me. Part of my job is to hire good people. If you're competent and you do your job, that's all I care about. Come back tomorrow, ready to work."

The woman nodded and gathered her things. After she had gone, Meg looked at Etienne. "She needed a job," was all that Meg said.

He studied her for long, silent moments. She looked at him, then looked away to the side. He noticed that she was fidgeting with the red leather band of her watch. Meg clearly wasn't as calm as she appeared to be.

"You needed to prove you were better than him, didn't you?" Etienne asked.

Now, she turned back to him in a rush. Her eyes flashed fire. "I *am* better than him," she said.

Etienne laughed. "Meg. Amazing, surprising Meg. You're not going to get a single argument from me.

There's no question in my mind that you're miles better than Alan is, was or ever could be. The question is…are you really going to be able to take working with the woman who was given your job the last time around? Without attempting to bring her down, I mean?" he asked gently. "Not that you'd do it consciously. I'm sure you'd be appalled by that, but…subconsciously, her presence has to sting a little."

"A little," Meg admitted. "But not as much as I might have once thought. After all, she and I have something in common. By rights we should actually bond over our dislike of Alan."

"Is that going to happen?"

"Probably not. I won't hold what happened against her, but the truth is that it was a dark day for me. She's a reminder of that. Bonding isn't going to take place."

"Still, you've just established yourself as a woman who knows how to be magnanimous and walks the walk. I'm betting that the people in the outer office are going to have an awful lot of questions."

"Yes, I know. I can hear the buzz already and…why not? I'd certainly be buzzing if I were in their shoes." She walked out the door and prepared to meet the barrage of questions.

And as she moved, Etienne realized one thing. By giving Meg this job, he had sentenced her to a somewhat lonely existence. Before, she had been a part of the masses. Now she was the one who handled all the decisions. At least she would handle all of them, alone, once he had gone. But being alone had been her curse all her life, and now he had sealed her fate. He *knew* what that place at the top could be like. It could make good people do bad things. It could doom a person to a loveless life.

Etienne swore softly in French. But that didn't change things. Meg was and might always be alone.

Except for her pets.

Except for her child.

Except for any man who might—finally—win her over, a man who would stay and be there for her, night and day. She said she didn't want a man. Would she ever change her mind? And what man would ever be good enough for her?

No man, Etienne thought. Not one. Lightning might turn out to be the perfect companion for Meg, after all. But no man as a husband didn't mean that there would never be a man in Meg's bed.

Etienne frowned. Where had that thought come from?

He didn't know. He didn't want to know. And he darn well wasn't going to pursue that line of thought, because the only thing he did know was that he wouldn't be the man in Meg's life.

A woman had loved him once. Her whole life she had loved him, but in the end, he had failed her.

He wouldn't do that to Meg, too.

So, what would he do?

Keep working for her, keep trying to save this place and these people she loved. Keep trying to make a difference in her life so that when he left she and her child and her world would be better off.

What was the next step?

Touch her, taste her. The thought leaped right in there. Meg Leighton was doing serious damage to his sanity. He wanted what Alan had thrown away. If he had needed any more proof that Alan had been a fool, that was it. Alan had walked away from the woman who made Etienne break out in night sweats.

* * *

What had she done, Meg wondered a few hours later. Paula Avery was young, blond, curvy and petite. A total cutie pie. The woman Alan Fieldman had chosen when he had gone looking for a hot, attractive, intelligent woman. The woman he had thrown Meg over for.

And Paula would be right there in front of Etienne every day of the week. He said he didn't want a woman, couldn't have one, but there was no way a man like Etienne was celibate. His kisses were too hot and demanding. He was most definitely a man who enjoyed women. And Meg had just hired a tasty dessert of a single woman who would be in the office every day.

Maybe she was doing it to punish herself for wanting him. "And maybe the stress of constantly striving to do better, to be better, to be different is starting to get to me," she muttered to herself.

Still, one thing was certain. Etienne had said he would leave. Other women had surely tried to get him to stay, and all of them had failed.

So, please, get Etienne out of your thoughts, she told herself. Don't even dare to remember his kisses.

But she woke in the middle of the night, remembering. She was going to have to do more to bring this relationship back into the realm of business partners and friends.

What could she do?

Something drastic.

CHAPTER TEN

"WHAT are you doing, Meg?" Etienne asked the next day.

Meg looked up at him. He was eyeing the green canvas bag she was carrying with curiosity.

"I'm planning something," she said, not hesitating lest she lose her nerve. "The thing is that everyone has been a bit stressed lately. With the way things are taking off with Fieldman's, it's kind of like watching an airplane trying to take off over a mountain range. You hope it will make it, but you're not completely sure that it can clear the upper peaks."

He grinned.

"Okay, I know why you're looking at me like that. The mountain analogy didn't quite cut it, but what I'm saying is still true in its own way, isn't it?"

"*Absolument*, Meg. *C'est vrai*. Of course. You're right."

Meg's breathing kicked up and she wanted to groan. She hated when he spoke French even though he was always careful to translate for her. *No, that was so wrong. She totally loved it when he spoke French, but it made her shake and burn inside so much that it scared her. French should be illegal or it should at least come with a warning label.*

"But I still don't understand," he said, nodding toward the bag.

"It's simple," she explained, dropping her bag of objects with a clatter. "Everyone is tense. We're beginning to snap at each other."

"I haven't heard you snapping at anyone."

She blushed. Okay, she was lying just a little. And she might even lie a little more. "On the inside I was snapping," she explained, and she quickly raised one hand. "Do *not*, under any circumstances, raise that eyebrow."

So, he didn't. He grinned, with those darn dimples that made her shiver.

"All right, Meg. What were you snapping about *on the inside*?"

She thought. Long. Hard. Trying to come up with a plausible answer. "I can't think of what it was right now, but there was something, and anyway, the whys and wherefores are beside the point. The point is that we're all under a lot of pressure. The expo is coming up in just two weeks and we need some way to let off steam. Hence, this."

She gestured toward the canvas bag she had been carrying.

"I see," he said. "And what is *this*?"

Meg pulled out a bat. "We're going to do something to help us get back to bonding and away from snapping. Something we can all do together as…as friends, but also as business partners. I understand that lots of businesses have teams of one sort or another and since there's a big field right outside our door, I thought that tomorrow at lunchtime, we could have a very short game of…of baseball."

"Of course. Do you play a lot of baseball, Meg?"

"Not a lot, no." In fact she had been horrible at all sports in school, but at least she knew the basics of baseball. And the equipment was simple, the field was there and she'd heard Jeff and some of the other men discussing the sport. This could be a good thing. It could take some of the edge she'd been feeling around Etienne off and bring her thoughts back to mere friendship. She hoped. "I thought you might captain one team and I would captain the other. I checked on the Internet and I know this isn't a very popular game in France but they do play it, don't they? There were eight major league baseball players in America who were born there, although…not for a while and not all even in the twentieth century. I would have chosen something else, like soccer…I mean your football…except I thought it would be best to have a low contact sport so that everyone could feel comfortable and not self-conscious. Not much touching in baseball, is there?" Oh, would someone please shut her up already?

"Except for the tagging part," he said. "That would be touching."

"But the baseball glove or at least having to have a ball in your hand when you tag a person would make it okay," she reasoned. "I was hoping this might be fun." Did she really sound wistful, hopeful, nervous? This had seemed like such a good idea when she'd thought of it, but now… She was terrible at sports. She'd been doing so well here, otherwise. This wasn't a good idea at all, was it?

"It's an excellent idea," Etienne said as if he'd been reading her mind. "And yes, people are getting a little tense. Let's do it."

"All right, I'll announce it today. That way everyone can

bring casual clothes. Shall we shorten the game to either three innings or an hour, whichever comes first?" She was beginning to feel better now. Organization was something she understood. Meg smiled and started to leave the room to make the announcement over the intercom.

"Meg, it *is* a great idea. And I think this might help with Paula, too."

She didn't even ask what he meant. No matter how much Meg had asked the people at Fieldman's to try and accept Paula, the woman was having a rough time of it. "I know. I think people are afraid that if they show her any kindness that they'll be disloyal to me."

"I can understand why they feel that way."

"I know. They think she hurt me and that I might still be hurting. I'll be putting her on my team to try to dispel that notion, if that's okay with you."

And Meg realized that while she wasn't heartbroken over Alan anymore, Paula did make her nervous in one very unacceptable way. Paula's eyes followed Etienne everywhere. She clearly had a crush...or more, and Paula was just as cute and tiny and as much of a show-stopper as she had been before. Meg hated that she even noticed that. Jealousy was not in her plans. She had no right to notice anything that went on between Etienne and Paula, so yes, Paula was going to be on her team, and she and Paula were going to work together.

"She's yours," Etienne said. "And Meg?"

"Yes?"

"Thank you. I've never played baseball before, but I have a feeling that this is going to be an unforgettable experience."

Meg had the feeling that it was, too. Had she really thought this through? Of course not, but heck, she had set it up and now she was going through with it. And she was going to make sure that Etienne enjoyed his first experience with baseball.

After all, what could really go wrong?

Etienne's team was in danger of losing, not because he didn't get the game. It was fairly simple, after all. And not because he was so inept. He'd discovered that he had a natural aptitude for hitting the ball with the bat, pitching and catching.

No, the problem was that he was worried about Meg. She seemed so determined to make sure that everyone had a good time, especially him, that she was running herself ragged. And also…she was just so very cute in her blue jeans and red T-shirt, with her inability to do anything that remotely resembled playing the game. She couldn't hit, throw or catch, but she was still making such a valiant effort that it was all but impossible not to want her to win.

He could tell that he wasn't the only one, either. Jeff was pitching now and while he was doing his best to give Meg easy pitches, she wasn't getting anywhere near the ball when she swung. Etienne looked at Jeff and the man seemed to be perspiring heavily.

"Jeff, don't look so worried. This is just a game," Meg said, propping her bat on the ground. But Etienne knew that Jeff didn't have any fear that Meg would fire him. She was the only person who hadn't managed to make contact with the ball today and the man just wanted it for her so badly.

"Now," Etienne said, hoping that his low tone would carry to Jeff but not to Meg.

Apparently it worked. "Are you sure, Meg?" Jeff

asked, but as he did, he threw the ball…straight toward her now stationary bat. It hit the wood and bounced back slightly into the field. A fair, playable ball.

"Run, Ms. Leighton!" Paula screeched.

Meg's eyes went wide. No one dove for the ball even though Lily, the catcher, could have easily reached it.

Meg glanced at her bat, at the ball, at the bat. She ran. Fast. Around first base, around second, nearing third as her team members jumped up and down and yelled and as the members of Etienne's team smiled and didn't do much of anything. But Etienne knew this deal wasn't completed yet. If Lily didn't go for the ball soon, Meg would be coming around third base and heading toward home plate with the ball lying not three feet away, right where it had fallen when it thudded off the bat. And while Jeff might have managed to surprise Meg with that hit, and while she hadn't yet noticed the opposition's in-activity, she was a highly intelligent woman. Eventually she would figure it out if no one made any effort at all. And Meg was not the kind of woman you let win. She would take it personally.

But what to do? Lily could still pick it up but Etienne wasn't sure that she would without some coaxing. As for him, he was playing short stop, not that close to the home plate. Still, he sprinted toward the base. Not too fast since he didn't want to beat her there, but not so slow that she would suspect.

As he moved, he looked at Meg. She was running, running, her pretty hair flying out behind her. Etienne was approaching the ball, but at this pace Meg would make it over the plate first. He could tag her just after the fact just as he wanted to and she would have scored for her team. He took his time when he scooped up the ball.

But Lily was standing near the plate, yelling Meg on and encouraging her. Suddenly Meg, fearing she would hit Lily, veered aside. She collided with Etienne, a bundle of soft skin and hair and elbows, one of which caught him in the side. Caught totally off guard, he took the hit full force and winced. Then, seeing she was falling down, he ignored his pain and reached for her. Too late. He missed. Meg fell to the ground, her body sliding on the dirt.

Etienne swore, in French, in English, even in Spanish.

"Meg! *Ma chère*, are you hurt?" Immediately he dropped to his knees and started examining her, running his hands over her. Her leg was bent slightly crooked and he couldn't tell if anything was broken or damaged. "Meg, talk to me. Say something. Say anything, all right?"

She gazed up into his eyes, blinking. "I… I ran into you. I didn't see you. Did I hurt you?"

Etienne closed his eyes. He let out a breath of relief. Then he opened his eyes and gazed down at her. He smiled. "Never."

Now her eyes were starting to clear. She was focusing. "Then…did I make it?"

No, she hadn't. Her arm was over her head, but the base was half an inch beyond, and he had touched her while holding the ball. By now he knew the rules of the game and that meant that she was out and hadn't scored for her team. Out of the corner of his eye, he saw Paula and Lily exchange a look.

Then Paula suddenly rushed forward and fell to her knees. "I… Years ago I started nursing school and I've had CPR training. Now I know that you think you feel all right, Ms. Leighton, but it just never hurts to make sure. Let me ask you a few questions just to be on the safe side. How many fingers am I holding up? What's your name? And what day is it?"

As she spoke, Etienne saw Lily stick her foot out and give a tiny kick.

"You seem okay," Paula said, "but that certainly gave me a scare. You could have hit your head."

When Paula rose and moved out of his way, Etienne saw that Meg's hand was now resting on the plate. He resisted the urge to smile.

"You made it," he whispered.

Meg suddenly sat up on her elbows and turned slightly, looking at the plate. When she turned back, there was a funny, crooked grin on her face. "Nice," she said.

And then she stared straight into his eyes. He was still kneeling beside her. One hand was still on her right leg. Both of them looked down to where their bodies were joined, and now it became something more than him trying to make sure she wasn't injured. The palm of his hand felt…warm. When she looked at him, her eyes looked languorous.

Someone—maybe Jeff—coughed, and Etienne slowly withdrew his hand. He helped Meg to her feet.

"I think game time is over," she said. "But it's been fun."

"You don't mean that."

She smiled, a smile that Etienne felt down to the soles of his shoes. "Yes, I do. I've always hated sports, but not today. I loved every minute."

"But, Meg," Edie said. "You can't give up now. Your team is still behind by one run."

Meg looked at Paula. "It's okay, isn't it?" She turned to the other members of her team, who seemed uncertain what to do. "It's not so much that we want to win," one of them said. "We just want *you* to win. No disrespect to you, Mr. Gavard."

"None taken," he said.

Meg's smile grew. "But I'm happy. I did win. In my own way, I did."

"Yeah," Paula said. "She made a run. That's winning."

And everyone took up the cry. Meg looked over her shoulder at Etienne. "Thank you," she said.

"For what?"

Meg shrugged. "You'd never even played baseball, but you went along with this impetuous plan of mine."

"I told you it was a great plan." And it had been. She had been right. There had been some sniping and tension during the past week, but here on this field where everyone wanted Meg to have her day in the sun, they had all joined together. Even Paula seemed to be taken into the fold.

"You are a man of many talents," Meg told him before joining Paula and Edie.

"I want you to know that I see how it is," he heard Paula saying. "And I wouldn't ever do anything that idiotic and cruel again. Not with you, that's for sure. He's yours free and clear."

And, even though they were farther away now, Etienne was almost certain that she heard Meg say. "Not mine."

He stared down at the baseball in his hand. Then he dropped it to the ground with a frown.

"Hey, at least we won," Jeff said.

But he hadn't, and he had no reason to complain. No reason at all. His relationship with Meg was what it was. There had been no hope for it from the start.

CHAPTER ELEVEN

THREE hours after the baseball game had concluded and a good two hours before the end of the workday, Meg looked up to see Etienne standing in the door of her office.

"Come on," he said. "Come with me."

"Where?"

"Home. And then out."

"Home? Now?"

"Yes. To change clothes."

"And then out? Do we have a meeting with anyone that I didn't hear about? A presentation? A dinner?"

"Yes, I'm taking you to an early dinner. Just us."

She tilted her head. "Is something wrong, Etienne?"

"No. Yes. You got hurt today, and I noticed that you're still limping even though you said you were fine. I'd simply try to send you home to bed but I understand that several people have already attempted that, and you've resisted. I suppose I could order you home, but…"

"You don't want to do that, because I'm in training to take over when you're gone, so you don't want to take my power away. Is that it?"

"Something like that."

"So you're taking me out to dinner."

"Yes, and then I thought I'd whisk you back home early and by…oh…seven o'clock you'd be in bed asleep."

She smiled. "That was very clever and conniving of you."

"It was, wasn't it," he said with a grin. "Too bad I'm not capable of lying to you."

"That's not such a bad thing, you know."

He shrugged. "Will you come with me, Meg?" And when he held out his hand to her that way, how could she say no?

She placed her hand in his. Why was it that every time he touched her, she felt it a little deeper and the longing got a little stronger? The pain when he finally left was going to be excruciating, but she didn't want to think about that. He was still here, right by her side. For now.

"I'm yours," she said.

Those gorgeous eyes turned dark and fierce. "Figuratively speaking," she added, trying not to blush. That had been a stupid, impetuous thing to say.

"Of course."

Of course. And in no time, he had her home. She changed into a white dress, an unusually colorless choice for her, but there was something serious about Etienne tonight, and she didn't want him to feel that he had to tease her about her bright colors the way he usually did.

What was wrong? Was it the upcoming anniversary of his wife's death? Or had she, Meg, failed to digest all that Etienne felt she needed to know?

In the weeks since they'd met, they had spent an hour or two of each day together while he coached her on all the aspects of business he felt she would need to know. And he had been amazingly well versed in the

American system. He possessed an abundance of knowledge about business law and labor and trade laws here. He taught her about stocks and bonds and retirement plans and employee insurance plans, about taxes and safety considerations and…everything, it had seemed. She had tried to digest as much as she could; she had taken books and files home every night, but her time had been limited and…she was worried and…

"Something's bothering you," she said. "Tell me." Just as if she had a right to invade his privacy.

But he didn't seem to notice that she had overstepped a boundary. "I let you get hurt today. I wasn't paying enough attention. If you had hit your head on the ground…if I had fallen on you and crushed you or caused you to break something vital, I…"

He turned to her and took her hands in his own. "I've pushed you too hard, Meg. You've been trying to be all things to all people, to prove that you can do it all, but you don't have to do it all. You shouldn't be forced to play a sport just to make everyone feel good. That day I came and lured you back here, I was pushy. I set a pace that was too driving. I've sapped your energy. You're limping."

His tone was angry, but she could see now that he wasn't angry at her but at himself. Still, she knew that the tragedy of his wife was at the heart of this. How could it not be? How did any man get past the guilt that she knew gnawed at him?

So what could she do? Meg rose up on her toes, wrapped her arms around his neck and kissed him. Solemnly. Slowly. And with fervor.

When she pulled back, she saw that Etienne looked dazed and stunned…and heated.

"Yes, I'd say I'm perfectly healthy," she said, a bit

breathlessly. "My heart started pounding just as it does whenever we kiss."

"Meg," he warned. "Don't do this. I don't have much self-control tonight."

"I don't, either," she said weakly, "so no, I won't do that again, but I just wanted you to know that I'm fine, Etienne. Really. And nothing is going to happen to me. You don't have to save me."

She looked away as she said that because yes, it was a bold and daring thing to say even though she was pretty sure that it was true. She finally got it.

Etienne saved things. He saved people. He did for everyone else what he hadn't been able to do for his wife.

That was why he was always so concerned about her. Oh, sure, he desired her, but then she was pretty sure that Etienne had a lot of experience desiring women. The concern thing clearly had its roots in his personal tragedy. It was up to her to free him from that. From now on, that was going to be her goal, to disentangle Etienne from her life so that if some little something ever did happen to her, he wouldn't blame himself.

That meant she needed to be less concerned about things. Publicly, that is.

"What?" she asked, realizing that she had missed his words while she'd been plotting.

"Here. Come inside, or would you rather sit on the patio? It's overcast, but I think we're safe from the rain for now," he said as he stopped walking. Meg looked up to see that they had walked to the entrance of Bistro Campagne.

Meg chose the patio. It was full of chatter and interesting people. The restaurant was a charming place, one she had never been to and the food was *magnifique*, as

Etienne said, but Meg was concentrating so hard on being bright and cheery and convincing Etienne that she was now the strongest, most learned, most accomplished, least likely person to ever suffer a tragedy or setback or even so much as a paper cut, that she missed most of the meal.

When they left the restaurant and began walking down the street, Etienne gave her a sideways smile. "You are an intriguing and infuriating woman, Meg Leighton."

That certainly got her attention. "Infuriating? In what way? I thought I was being rather pleasant tonight."

"*Exactement.* You're being the brightest, most falsely cheerful person ever. It is an act a man who didn't even know you could see right through. And I happen to know you. Well," he said in a way that made her feel that he knew intimate things about her. She felt the tingle rip slowly through her body.

"I was that obvious, was I?"

"Well, maybe not that obvious, but as I said, I know you."

He did, but…not everything. He certainly couldn't know just how much his words, his accent, his dimples, the way he looked at her or touched her affected her. She was totally incapable of managing her feelings when Etienne was near.

"You were trying to distract me so that I wouldn't worry," he accused. "Weren't you?"

She couldn't lie to him. Much. "Maybe a little," she admitted. "But what about you?" she said. "I happen to know you, too, and I know very well that I did not score a run today."

Etienne looked as if she had taken that baseball bat and physically walloped him with it. "Meg…" he began.

"Etienne," she said, turning to face him and standing her ground. "You know you won't lie to me."

"I won't."

"What was Lily doing behind me when Paula was asking me all those questions? I heard a sound, and later when we went inside I saw that things looked a bit…disturbed around the base."

"You don't seriously think I would say something bad about Lily, do you?"

"It wouldn't be a bad thing. Don't you think I know that everyone felt sorry for me because I was such a stinker at the game and that they all wanted me to at least have one drop of success? That's true, isn't it?"

He reached out and brushed her cheek, and sensation shot through her. "If it's true, it was a good thing, Meg. They love you."

"But it was cheating."

He laughed. "Not when both teams are rooting for the same person. Besides, it broke the ice for Paula. In the end, I'd say several good things happened there. Everyone worked together, they all went away happy and now people are speaking to Paula so she can concentrate on her work more."

"If she wasn't concentrating on her work before, it was because she has a crush on you."

"That's just because she's lonely. It will pass."

"Etienne?"

"Yes?"

"Thank you for trying to make me believe that I don't suck at baseball. I knew it wasn't true, but it was nice to be forced to pretend for a while."

"So you'll let them continue to believe you believe?"

"If it will keep everyone happy, I will. And…when

I said that I won today, well, I did. Maybe I didn't break
my long running record of never scoring a run, but the
fact that people cared enough to make me want to
believe that I had…that was winning for me. So no, I
won't say anything."

"You're going to be so good at this, Meg. You have
the love and loyalty of the people who work for you. I
didn't teach you that."

She smiled. "But you are responsible for this." She
looked down at herself. "Daniel sent someone to my
house to teach me how to apply makeup and do my
nails. A woman showed up and gave me all kinds of instructions on the best clothing to, quote, accent my
physical features. She even showed me how to walk
with more confidence so that I would 'wear my clothes
well' and they wouldn't wear me. I know that was all
your doing."

"Window dressing," he said. "Polish. So…since we're
discussing clothing, I notice that you, Meg Leighton, are
dressed all in white tonight. No other color. Meg?"

She shrugged. "It seemed to fit the mood."

Etienne frowned. "But it's not you. Don't try to
change yourself in order to accommodate someone else's
mood." He turned the corner. It wasn't the way to his car.

"Where are we going?"

"Somewhere… I know there was a man the other day
when I was out this way… Here," Etienne said, satisfaction coloring that rich, deep voice of his. He stopped
before a flower vendor, picked out a nosegay of wine-
red roses and handed them to Meg.

When she took them, Etienne moved back two steps.
"Yes. All's right with the world now. Red. It's you.
Passionate. Colorful. Exciting."

She laughed. "Is there another woman standing behind me that you're talking about? No one has ever said that I was exciting."

"Well, now they have. I have. And you know that I don't lie to you."

They had backtracked and were on their way back to the car when the threat of rain became a reality. A light mist began to fall and quickly became harder.

Automatically it seemed, Etienne put his arm around Meg and pulled her under the shelter of an awning.

"Wait here," he told her as he rushed back out into the rain, which was coming down harder now.

"Etienne, you're getting soaked," she yelled, but he paid her no mind. Instead he ducked into a nearby hotel. Through the glass doors, she could see him speaking to the doorman, gesturing to the man. Then he reached into his pocket and pulled out his wallet. Within seconds he was running back to her carrying a large black umbrella. He flipped it open and when he reached the awning, he took her hand and pulled her under the umbrella with him.

"The man sold you one of the hotel's guest umbrellas?" she asked, laughing as Etienne wrapped one arm around her waist to hold her close and keep her out of the rain. "I'll bet he's not supposed to do that. Did you have to give him half your fortune?"

"Meg," Etienne lectured. "Are you making fun of me for trying to keep you from getting soaked?"

Suddenly she stopped. She turned in his arms and faced him. "Not at all. I like the way you identify a problem and then immediately identify a solution. You're a magic man, *mon cher*. Is that how you say it?"

But he was still holding her against him, the flowers

crushed between their bodies. "That's how you say it, my Meg. And no, I'm not a magic man. Just a man. A man who has to do this. Right now."

His mouth came down on hers. He pulled her closer still. She dragged her arm, flowers and all, free and looped it around his neck, trying to get closer to him.

The rain came down, and Etienne's kisses became deeper, more demanding.

Meg tilted her head and gave and gave. And took and took. She tasted him, she savored him, she wished this moment would never end, that they could stay beneath this cocoon of an umbrella in the rain forever. Alone. Just the two of them. With nothing else to come between them.

But in the distance a car horn honked. People yelled at each other, they laughed. More traffic noises intruded, and the streetlights came on.

The real world returned, and in the real world Etienne was a man who might want kisses but didn't want more. He could have any woman he wanted, but he wanted none. At least not for more than this.

And Meg realized how unprotected her heart was. She was in grave danger of doing something very unhealthy to herself. Something she had sworn not to do again. Fall for a man who would, ultimately, break her heart. Etienne might not want to do that to her, but it would be done nonetheless.

And when it happened, he would know. It would send him to a very bad place, emotionally. She needed to keep that from happening. Somehow she needed to be a woman who dealt in solutions. Emotional solutions.

Gently, carefully, reluctantly, Meg eased herself away. "That was…very nice. You're exceptionally good at that. But I suppose you know that. It was…a very ef-fective lesson."

He frowned. He growled. "You know that was no lesson."

"I know you didn't mean it to be one, but neverthe-less it was. If I'm going to be doing business with the big boys, I have to know how to go one-on-one with them. I'm assuming that now and then there might be temptation. I need to know how to…to walk away from it, don't I?"

For several seconds Etienne didn't answer. He was looking angry, angrier than she had ever seen him. "You definitely need to know how to walk away from temp-tation. Especially temptation that is bad for you."

She just couldn't do it. No matter the need, even to save Etienne in the end, she just couldn't pretend in this way. Instead she touched him on the sleeve. "I didn't mean it. You're not bad for me. You know how much you've done for me, but…this…this part of the two of us…it's only going to hurt us both in the end. I don't want to hurt you."

"Dammit, Meg, I'm the one who's supposed to say that. I pulled you into this. I get to be the protector."

She placed her palm across his lips and slowly shook her head. "You can't be my protector, Etienne. You can't save me. In the long run we both know that that job can't be yours. And I don't want you to regret it. I want you to enjoy your time with me."

"I do," he promised. "I am. I will."

"For now," she whispered. "We still have some time left. And we have rain and red flowers and a beautiful umbrella. Let's walk in the rain."

"Impetuous," he said and the word was a caress. "But your leg. I've walked you too far already."

"I don't even feel it anymore," she promised. And it was true. For now all she felt was the need to walk with this man who had changed her life so much. For this one moment she would not worry about tomorrow and just enjoy this man and this simple pleasure. Who knew what tomorrow would bring?

CHAPTER TWELVE

ETIENNE knew that he was losing control where Meg was concerned. There was just something about her that made him forget all the things he needed to remember. Yes, he was a successful businessman, but he had failed in his personal life and had hurt those he should have taken better care of. He just could not risk failing or hurting anyone else, especially not Meg.

Bright, beautiful Meg who deserved that loving, secure home surrounded by children that she desired. The thought of interfering with those dreams of hers in any way just wasn't something he could face. He'd hate *himself* if he caused her any pain. So he had to stop thinking about her all the time, stop spending so much time with her before he did any irreversible harm to her.

How was he going to do that?

Keep it low-key, Gavard, he told himself. *Keep it all business.* The way Meg wanted things. Couldn't he do that much for her?

With that as his goal, he pressed himself to concentrate on the company and drove himself around the clock. He almost thought that he was making progress when he had gone a whole week without touching Meg.

Yes, it had been a hellish week. He missed Meg so much that he felt crazy and hot, so much so that he hadn't even been paying attention to the calendar and that hated day looming before him. He wanted nothing more than to go slamming into Meg's office and just...look at her, be near her. But somehow he managed to stay away. With a gargantuan effort he kept his distance. He was even beginning to think that he might have himself under control a bit.

Until he looked up one day and found her standing in the doorway to his office. Her brown eyes were bright and fierce.

Immediately, as if he couldn't help himself, he rose and went to her. "Meg, what's wrong?" He reached out and took her hands.

She hesitated.

"Meg? Tell me."

She shook her head. "It's you."

"Me? What did I do?"

"You're just doing too much for us. You're pushing yourself too hard. You've been here day and night and you're looking tired. It's occurred to me that there's a lot more at stake here than just Fieldman's and all of us who work here."

Etienne frowned at that. "What do you mean?"

"I mean you. Your reputation. You've been working so hard for us, but:...what about you? You've been very nice about not pointing out to all of us that you have a reputation to uphold. Whether we...*I*, do a good job and cut a good image could affect you. And you haven't even said anything. Is that why you've been so upset lately?"

It almost broke Etienne's heart that Meg was worrying about him. "I haven't been upset, *ma chère*."

She crossed her arms. "You promised me truth."

"All right, the truth is that I've given no thought whatsoever to my reputation." He offered up a smile.

Meg frowned harder. "Then the reason you've been upset—"

"I didn't say I was upset."

"Etienne, did I ever tell you that I'm a very visual person? I need to see things in order to get them straight, but once I see them, everything falls into place. You've been preoccupied and you've been frowning a lot. Your eyes…"

"My eyes?"

She glanced up then and blushed. "Well, never mind your eyes, but something is wrong. I know it."

What to say? He was not going to bring up his concerns about hurting or disappointing her. He had promised that they would be friends and all business. The fact that he was having trouble sticking to the script was his problem and not hers.

"Is it… Etienne, I know this is nosy. And it's none of my business but…I mentioned earlier that I read about you and your life on the Internet. I'm sure this is a difficult time of the year for you. I don't want to be insensitive. If you'd like… If you need time away, Edie and Jeff and the rest of us won't let the place collapse while you're gone and I can promise you that we… Etienne, you've made things easier for us. I wish I could make this easier for you somehow…"

Her voice faltered and Etienne realized that she was all but ripping off the button on her skirt, twisting it nervously.

Carefully he covered her hand with his own, stilling her.

"I don't want you worrying about me," he said.

"But…"

"Meg, my problems aren't yours. And don't worry. I'm used to dealing with problems. It's what I do."

She got that stubborn look in her eyes. "Maybe, but you're still human. When July 18 rolls around, I'll expect you to take the day off."

The fact that she had the day right hit him in the solar plexus. The fact that she hadn't backed down and was still insisting that he tend to his needs…amazed him.

"Are you giving me orders, Meg?"

She pushed her chin up. "No, I'm not. I'm just being your friend. You had a wife. You had a child on the way. You get to be human and take time out to mourn them."

But he never really had. He reached out suddenly, took Meg's hands and pulled her to him. "It's not that simple, Meg. I wasn't a good husband to Louisa. The child was a duty for her, another accomplishment to be checked off the list for me. Had I been paying any attention to her at all, we might have discovered her condition and avoided the pregnancy, but I wasn't even thinking about her. And later, when I made that statement to my mother, I didn't even think about the fact that I was, intentionally or not, placing some of the blame for Louisa's and our son's death on her. I failed my wife, my child and my family, so no, I don't allow myself to mourn. If I didn't do the right things while they were with me it's too late to do them now. There's no need to worry about me, though, Meg. Work may have been what killed my marriage, but it's also what keeps me sane now."

He looked up and saw that Meg's eyes were wet. Two thick tears hung on her lashes.

"I thought that you never cried."

"I don't," she said, dashing the tears away. "I'm not crying. I'm angry."

"At what?"

"At you. Why do you expect yourself to be so... perfect, so responsible for everyone and everything? That's wrong. People should be responsible for their *own* happiness, but... No, I'm not going to say any more. It's totally wrong for me to be telling you all this when I have no idea what it's like to live in your shoes. I never can keep my mouth shut."

"I've never asked you to."

She shook her head. "I know that. I'm trying to learn to do that myself, but I'm still a work in progress."

He smiled sadly. "Don't worry about me, Meg. My distance lately hasn't been because I'm morose but because...well, you know that I desire you. I don't want to leave here with regrets."

"You're still worried that you'll hurt me? Well, I still say that my emotional state is my own problem. You can't be responsible because I won't allow it. Our deal was that you should teach me, not that you should wrap me up in tissue paper and put me in a box so I won't get broken."

"Do you feel that I've fallen down on the job? Have I failed to teach you something you think you need to know? You already know most of what's necessary to keep this company running."

"I don't know. What more *do* I need to learn?"

Not much, Etienne conceded, but the fact that he'd been upsetting Meg with his attempt to protect her from himself was unacceptable. She had enough on her plate. He didn't want her worrying about him.

"Perhaps...we need to take a stab at some dance lessons?"

Her eyes widened. "You're kidding, right? I need to know how to dance, too?"

"You told me that you only knew how to do the polka."

"And I don't even do that right, if you remember correctly. I was leading you the whole time. Plus, remember all those classes I told you that I took? You're talking about a woman who couldn't even master the basics of how to fall gracefully."

Etienne grinned. "I'm not going to let you fall, Meg."

She smiled back at him. "Okay, but I can't imagine why this would be an essential skill. Will we be dancing in France?"

He didn't want to lie to her. "Definitely." He would make very sure of that. Especially since what was needed right now was some dancing, some levity, a release of the tension they'd all been subjected to.

"Where should we go?"

He grinned. "The outer office."

"In front of everyone?"

"They can dance, too."

She put her head back and laughed at that. "Oh, they're going to love that. Somehow I don't think that I can simply tell everyone that we're expanding their job descriptions again."

"Don't worry, Meg," Etienne whispered. "Just tell them that we're having recess. Tell them that it will help you. They'll do anything you ask."

"They'll do anything you ask, too."

He raised a brow.

"Really," she said. "You may not have noticed but they've latched on to you as one of their own. They trust you now."

Which made Etienne more than a little nervous. No matter what Meg said, he *was* responsible for this company, for her and for what happened at that expo.

Betray Meg or fail the company and he would be destroying lives. Again.

"So, you think they won't report me to the labor union if I ask them to tango?"

"As long as you remove the thorns from the roses they hold in their teeth, I think they'll be amused by the diversion."

But, of course, it wasn't that simple.

"We need music," Meg said, "and something to play it on."

After an announcement and a quick search, it just so happened that Jeff had a portable MP3 player in his car with some tiny speakers that would plug into it.

"Sometimes I like to go to the park at lunch," he explained. "You may not like my taste in music, though."

Jeff's taste in music ranged from hip hop to jazz with a little rock thrown in. Trying to find something that a person could ballroom dance to was a challenge, but Harold managed to locate some slow love songs. "Ooh, this one sounds hot!" Harold said, which made Jeff's ears turn red.

"I don't know how that got there," he said.

Etienne chuckled. "Just keep repeating that, my friend," he said. "Not that anyone will believe it."

"Jeff, it's a really nice song," Meg argued. "You play that when you have a woman with you and I guarantee she'll melt."

Which made Etienne sit up and take notice. He wanted Meg to melt for him.

But, of course, that wasn't what he was supposed to be thinking about. "Let's get some space," he directed. Together everyone pushed the desks out of the way.

Then he turned to see a small sea of expectant faces

turned his way. "Partner up," he directed. "Grab the person next to you, no matter what sex. We'll switch for the next song."

There was some giggling as people paired up with colleagues.

"We'll begin with a simple waltz. If you haven't done much of this before, then this is how the dance proceeds. You place your hand on her, or his, waist like this," Etienne said, and he slowly slid his palm around Meg's waist.

Immediately he was aware of her softness, how she fit him and how his heart pounded when he stared down into her eyes. "She places her hand on your shoulder. And then you take her hand in yours," he said, his voice thick in his own ears.

As he called out instructions, Jeff started the music and the group began to move, but Etienne was only aware of Meg, of looking into her eyes, of twirling with her around the floor.

"You're very good," she said, her voice so soft he nearly had to lean close to hear.

"Years of practice. It's second nature." But it wasn't. Not with her. The waltz had never seemed so exhilarating, so meaningful, so short.

The music ended. "Switch," Jeff said, and he headed straight toward Meg.

Etienne's hand tightened on hers for a second, but then he released her, ceding his place to the other man. The one who would stay. Etienne hadn't failed to notice Jeff's interest in Meg. She might find happiness with him.

But not yet. Not today.

Etienne led them through a series of mini lessons in various ballroom dances, but when they came to the tango he claimed Meg as his own again.

"Last one," he said. "And for this one, Meg is mine."

He looked up into Jeff's stubborn eyes and felt a twinge of sympathy for the man. Also a trace of guilt. He had seniority here and it wasn't fair to pull rank.

But he did it anyway. "There might be dancing in Paris," he explained to the man, even though he was pretty sure that there wouldn't be an opportunity for anything quite like this. He just wanted the chance to dance with her, to be with her.

He pulled her into his arms, swirled her into the dance.

Meg was obviously new to the dance; she was awkward, very self-conscious and totally charming. "If I step on your feet you'll forgive me, won't you?" she asked. "And not yell out too loud?"

"I'll swallow the pain," he promised. "And love every minute."

Which, of course, made her chuckle in that low, husky way she had that made his nerves sing.

They moved through the dance, circling each other, twirling, gazes connected, not paying attention to anyone else in the room until the music reached its crescendo. "Now dip," Etienne directed, and he lowered Meg into his arms, ending up only a breath from her lips.

"And up," he whispered, pulling her back into his arms as the music died away.

By then everyone was laughing and breathing heavily. "Do you do this kind of thing at every company you reclaim?" Edie asked.

"This was Meg," he said. "All Meg."

So no, he would never do this again. The sands of time were running out. In just over a week, she would walk out of his life.

And he would have to take it. There was no other way.

CHAPTER THIRTEEN

THE days were spinning by, the expo was almost here, Meg and Etienne were leaving the next day and the company was developing a slow, quiet hum of efficiency rather than the awkward thump, thump of a car driving along minus one wheel.

Still, with the prospect of speaking before an international audience, Meg should have been petrified. That had been her modus operandi for most of her life. Stay out of the spotlight. Don't attract attention. Hide your defects. But, that just wasn't happening this time. The scar, the weight, the awkwardness and tendency to speak her mind too freely…those things just weren't bothering her. Etienne had worked his magic and made her feel unique. Whether it was true or not, she felt it and that was really all that mattered.

He'd changed her life, and she was grateful, but…

"What are you going to do when he's gone?" Edie asked her one day.

Meg froze. "I don't know what you mean."

"Meg, this is Edie. I've known you forever. You follow him with your eyes. You watch for him when he's not here. You're falling in love with him."

Meg opened her mouth to deny it, but this *was* Edie. No point in trying to pretend.

"It doesn't matter. He's not a staying kind of guy. He doesn't want children. I'm not even sure he could deal with the cats, but mostly it's just…he's not a man a woman should allow herself to fall in love with."

"And yet you have."

"Not yet. Not completely," Meg said. "I've known he was off-limits from the start, so I've been careful." Or as careful as she was capable of being. "But I *will* miss him." Desperately.

And more than that, she would worry about him. For all he had done for them, for all that she knew he would move on and do the same for another company, maybe hitch up with another woman such as herself, he was essentially alone. He had built himself an emotional prison of constant movement where he wasn't allowed to make lasting connections.

Still, it was what he wanted, and maybe, Meg realized, it was the first time in his life he was able to have what he wanted. From what he'd said, it sounded as if his younger years had been lived according to the family plan. His marriage had been expected, an heir had been expected, and trying to twist himself into a pretzel to do the expected things had hurt a lot of people. One of the people most damaged had been Etienne, though he would never admit that.

But Meg did. She also admitted that his choice to live his life alone was one she had to respect. It wasn't the kind of thing she would choose—she did want those babies—but if being alone and always on the move in his bid to help failing companies brought Etienne peace and made him happy… She *so* wanted him to be happy.

So, she pasted on a smile and ignored the pain in her heart. She still had him for a few more days before she had to give him up.

Etienne looked on in amusement as Meg squirmed in her seat on the plane. "Can you believe that you and I are going to France?" she asked.

He smiled. "I think I can."

"Okay," she said with a grin. "I suppose that was a silly question. *You* jet around all the time, but I've never been anywhere, least of all France."

"I hope you like it."

She gave him a tap on the arm. "As if I couldn't. I'm going to love it." She squirmed some more.

"Are you worried?" he asked. "Meg, you're not worried, are you? Because I've explained that you're going to be fantastic, haven't I?"

"Yes, you have."

"And…"

"And, has it ever occurred to you that you may be a tiny bit biased? I'm your creation, after all."

Etienne frowned and turned in his seat. "You're no one's creation. You're one of a kind."

She laughed. "Let's hope that's a good thing."

It was. A very good thing. And everyone would recognize that at the expo. Etienne had put more effort into Fieldman's than he had ever put into any company and he knew it was because he wanted to make sure that Meg was set up with her heart's desire when he left. That company was her home, and he wanted it to thrive and grow, for her sake. He wanted her to have everything she wanted out of life.

Including those children. Meg, he knew, would never

choose to have a child simply out of some misguided sense of duty the way he had. Like some task that had to be accomplished.

Regret hit him, but he ignored it. This wasn't about him. It was about Meg and her happiness.

"You're going to shine," he assured her.

"I will," she promised, and he felt a twinge of concern. She wasn't just doing this for him, was she?

"Where's Lightning?"

"I left her with Edie. And Jeff took Pride and Prejudice, although he agrees with you. He said that they were both guys and they needed more manly names. I expect to come back and find that he's teaching them how to pick up felines."

Etienne laughed. "Jeff's a good man. He'd make sure that everyone ended up happy, I'll bet." He had the feeling that Jeff might be looking for a mate for more than the cats, too, a fact that sent an arrow straight into Etienne's heart. But he had no business going there. Jeff *was* a good man, one who wouldn't destroy a woman's self-esteem and lose her love by leaving her alone all the time. Or by valuing her child more for what it meant to the family name rather than for the joy a child could bring.

Meg had said she wanted to raise a family alone, but that didn't mean there wouldn't be men in her life. She might even change her mind if the right man came along. And if Jeff was the man who could make Meg happy, then he would do his utmost to be happy that the man was there for her, Etienne promised himself.

But for now, Meg was still with him, and he was going to savor every moment he had left with her.

So, the next morning, after she'd had time to rest up from the flight, he was at her door.

She opened it wearing some sort of slender, red dress that emphasized her shape and showed her pretty knees.

"I don't remember that dress," he told her.

She gave him a brilliant smile that made him want to lean close. "I bought this myself. I wanted to do some shopping while you were still around to tell me whether I had made a mistake...or not."

He tucked a finger beneath the long, slender deep-cut collar, sliding his way down the length of the cloth. "Very definitely an *or not*. No question. It suits you, very much."

"Well, there you go," she said as Etienne came into her room and she began to comb her hair. "My day just started off right. Edie told me it worked, but Edie is always nice about what I wear and she doesn't have much better taste than I do. You, however, are an expert."

"On some things," he agreed, watching the hypnotic movement of her arm as she stroked the comb through her curls. "Not on everything."

"What things don't you know enough about?" she wondered, turning to face him.

"Cats?" he suggested.

"Okay, cats. I take it you never had any growing up. How about a dog?"

"Not a dog, either."

"No pets?" she asked. Etienne noticed that there was a stray curl that Meg had missed. It lay partially across her cheek. He wanted to brush it aside with his fingertips.

"No pets," he said, continuing to study that curl and the one next to it that swirled down, just touching the hollow of her throat. That very sexy little hollow made for a man's lips.

"None?" Meg asked with that sad voice that told him

she was moving directly into her "I want to fix things, I want to help you" mode.

He cleared his throat, tried to ignore the need to touch her and managed a smile to reassure her. "Don't look so sad. I had no clue I was missing anything. My mother simply feared animals, and she didn't like having their fur on her clothing or the furniture at Mont Gavard."

"Wow. Your home is on a mountain?"

"Sounds grand doesn't it?" he asked with a laugh. "But the mountain is really just a small hill. It's a pretentious name, but a beautiful estate nonetheless."

"You must miss it when you're away."

Those beautiful eyes of hers looked suddenly sad.

"I'm not a puppy or a kitten, Meg. You can't save me. And anyway, I don't need saving. There's no reason to be sad about the ancestral home because I'm away from it so much. The truth is that it's far too big for one person, so I've only been there once or twice since my mother died."

"How long ago was that?"

"Almost two years. There's a skeleton crew that takes care of the grounds and keeps things running smoothly."

"It sounds like a lovely place."

"I could show it to you if you'd like."

"Would you do that? I mean…I wouldn't want to ask you to do something you didn't feel like doing. You don't have to play the host if it makes you sad or brings back unhappy memories."

He thought about that. He *had* been sad the last time he was there. His mother had loved Mont Gavard, and the place had seemed to be missing an essential element without her, but…

"I didn't live there with Louisa. The vastness of the

estate intimidated her, and my mother was never happier than when people were admiring her home. I think she'd be happy that someone was showing an interest. But…"

"See, there is a problem. I shouldn't have asked."

Etienne brushed a finger across her nose. "Stop it. There isn't a problem in the way you're thinking. I just… We only have two days before the expo. If you go to Mont Gavard, that will only leave you one day to see Paris."

She looked at him with that clear, direct gaze of hers. "There's only one Paris, and I might never get the chance again, but lots of people see Paris. How many see Mont Gavard? I'll see what I can of Paris in a day. I'd like to see where you grew up."

"Why?"

She hesitated. "You're an interesting man. Your home must be an interesting place."

"Flattery will get you there, sweet Meg. I would love to show you my home," he said. "Come on." He took her hand. And then, because he couldn't seem to help himself, he stopped and smoothed that curl back behind her ear.

She shivered, and his self-control wavered even more. With the greatest of difficulty he managed not to kiss her. He had a feeling that these next few days were going to be very difficult, very wonderful and far too short. He hoped that when they ended their time together he would handle things right. He wanted Meg to be happy when he had gone, with no regrets.

Visiting Mont Gavard was probably a very good idea, after all. Despite the way things had been between him and his mother at the end, he had always loved the place. There was a serenity about it that reminded him of the way Meg made him feel when she was smiling.

That was a good thing, because while most of the time Meg seemed to be blessed with bravado, there were those moments such as the one when she asked him about her dress, when he realized how much she disliked being on display. How nervous and self-conscious she still was when she had to face strangers.

At the expo, he would be the only familiar face in the crowd. And for the two days they were there, she would be very much on display. A day at Mont Gavard might be just the thing to help her relax before all the madness to come.

He was going to make it a priority to help her relax, second only to his priority to keep his hands and his lips off her.

That would be a tough one, because every time Meg opened her mouth…or smiled…or laughed…or just existed, he wanted to kiss her.

Meg was thinking fast. Tomorrow was the anniversary of the day Etienne had lost his wife and child three years ago. She probably shouldn't have asked to see his home. No matter what he had said, there had to be some residual melancholy lingering about the place, memories of things gone by that could never come again because the key players were gone.

When she had first discovered that he was going to be running Fieldman's she had done an Internet search on his background and discovered that his reclamation business had grown much more intense after the tragedy of his wife and child. Even though he hadn't said so, she had seen firsthand how Etienne threw himself into work when something was bothering him. She also knew that he had arranged this two day lull before the demands of the expo so she would have time to rest up after the flight and have time to relax and prep herself.

But what was good for her was probably the exact opposite of what was good for Etienne at this moment. He needed activity, something to take his mind off things, a distraction.

"Well, I've certainly been called that more than once in my lifetime," Meg muttered to herself. And not necessarily in a good way, either, but for the first time ever, she was glad of that.

For the next two days she was going to devote herself to making sure that Etienne had no time to dwell on his sorrows, no time even to think, and no reason at all to regret that he had taken Meg on as a project.

She was going to do her darnedest to distract the man and to keep him busy, even if he ended up sorry that he had ever met her. She was pretty darn sure that he would spend at least some of the next two days beating up on himself if he had time to think about the past, so she was just going to have to deal with the fact that a sacrifice was needed here. There was no one around to care about Etienne's state of mind but her, and…she cared. A great deal.

So, that night, Meg sat down and made a list of places she intended to drag Etienne to, things she intended to ask him to show her, questions she intended to ask him, even general points of conversation to pursue should she need a desperation move.

She was a woman on a mission.

CHAPTER FOURTEEN

ETIENNE had chosen not to drive today. Instead he'd had Carl bring the limo to the hotel, so he and Meg were seated next to each other when they came over the rise and first caught a glimpse of Mont Gavard.

It had been a long time since he'd seen it, and the familiar rolling lush green fields, followed by the double rows of trees forming a canopy over the long driveway had him sitting up straighter. When the limo emerged from the tunnel of trees, the familiar pink brick of the L-shaped three story house with its white stone trim and cupola was revealed.

"It's… Oh, my, it's beautiful and so much larger than I had envisioned it," Meg said. "And…did you say that there was a skeleton crew taking care of the place? Because those shrubberies are perfect, there's not a weed in sight, and the flower beds, what I can see of them, are spectacular."

"It's an excellent crew," Etienne conceded with a smile.

"I can tell. Can I meet them? And…will you show me the rest of the gardens? And…"

She glanced down at something in her hand. "And isn't there a pond? I looked up Mont Gavard on the Internet and it said there was a pond."

Without a thought, Etienne reached over and took the piece of paper from her.

"Don't," she said.

But it was too late. He had already looked. "Meg," he said gently. "Don't you trust me to show you everything?"

She nodded. "Yes, yes I do."

"Then why the list?"

That adorable chin rose just a touch. He could tell she was going to get stubborn on him. "I just…like lists."

"Nothing wrong with lists," he agreed, "but this one seems incredibly long. I'm pretty sure that even if we had a month we wouldn't be able to do everything on it."

"Not everything on the list is a thing to do. Some of them are talking points."

He laughed out loud. "Meg, have you and I ever run out of things to say to each other?" No, they hadn't, he thought. "Don't you think I'm capable of carrying on an intelligent conversation with you? Especially about the place where I lived for most of my life?"

Her brown eyes opened wide. "Of course. I would never insult you by insinuating that you couldn't carry on a conversation with me. I love talking with you."

Warmth slipped right through him. "Then, Meg…"

"I just want to keep you busy today. And tomorrow," she said. "To distract you. That's all."

"Ah, I see."

"You weren't supposed to see. I was supposed to be talkative and demanding."

"Oh, I like that," he said. "Especially the demanding part. Go ahead. Demand something of me, Meg," he coaxed.

And suddenly, his talkative Meg seemed to have

nothing to say. She simply…looked at him. "I can't. I can't…even think."

He slid his hand beneath her hair, curling his palm around her neck. "Then don't think," he said. "I know what day it is, but don't try to distract me. Don't feel you have to be my keeper today. Let's just be. The two of us. We'll take it slow. I'll show you my favorite places. We'll talk when we like and we won't talk when we don't want to. You don't have to worry about me, Meg. I like spending time with you. You're already distraction enough. Come on, we're here. Walk with me."

She nodded. When they left the limo, she took his hand, and he led her around this place where he had spent so many years. Meg, his boisterous, talkative, sometimes outrageous Meg was very quiet.

"Are you all right?" he asked.

She frowned. "That was supposed to be my job. Asking you that…or *not* asking you that. I didn't want to remind you, and look at this… I had barely arrived when you got me to blurt out the whole truth. I'm hopeless where you're concerned."

Something about that very fact and the way she said it turned Etienne warm inside.

"You're not hopeless. You're adorable."

"You have so got to be kidding."

"I have so *not* got to be kidding, Meg." He kissed her nose, only allowing himself that much. "Adorable. Now, come on, I want to show you what I used to do when I needed to be alone."

He took her hand and led her down the path, past the patio where his parents had first told him that his father wasn't going to live much longer and all that would be expected of him. This was the place where he had dashed his mother's hopes of him ever fulfilling the Gavard legacy. His chest tightened as he thought of those times, but he concentrated on Meg. He squeezed her hand and she looked up at him with a smile that made him forget everything but her. Had the woman really had some plan to keep him so busy that he wouldn't have time to think about Louisa and his child? That was so…so very Meg.

She was so giving, amazing, vulnerable. If he hurt her…ever…

He wouldn't. It wasn't allowed.

Instead he led her to the water and a small boat that was kept there. "It's a shallow pond," he told her. "Are you game?"

"Is Paris in France?" she asked, climbing into the boat. She had worn slacks and a vivid red blouse. Now, perched in the small boat, she was like a brilliant, beautiful poppy that had been cast on the water.

He rowed around to the back side of the small island in the middle of the pond. Willow trees lined the shore here, their fronds trailing in the water. It was peaceful, quiet, secluded.

"I liked this place because no one ever looked for me here. Despite having a pond, my parents weren't fond of water. Now," he said. "You were going to distract me. Tell me all the things you were going to do."

She gave him a look. "I'm not ashamed of any of them."

"Good. You shouldn't be. I'm moved that you would make such an effort for me."

Meg shook her head. "You've certainly gone out of your way for me. That means so much to me."

Her voice dropped and he wanted nothing more than to lean forward and kiss her. Instead he tried to distract himself.

"So what was on the list?"

"I was going to ask you to give me a tour of the house and a tour of the grounds. If necessary, I was going to have you ask your cook to give me a list of your favorite recipes. I thought that might take a while. If necessary, I would have had you introduce me to all the staff here, take me to the nearest town, introduce me to the townspeople, and if worse came to worse, I was willing to go so far as to ask to see your stable of cars. I hear there's a very well stocked garage here."

"You have an interest in cars?"

"Not a bit, but if you do, that's all that matters."

"And I stopped you from doing all those things. That's probably a good thing, especially because you're not even interested in cars," he teased. "Meg?"

She looked up, waiting.

"This," he said, gesturing to the boat. "You wouldn't have lied to me and expressed an interest in going out on the boat with me if you really had no interest, would you?"

She took a deep breath. "Ordinarily, no, but today I would have done pretty much anything."

"So, you don't like boats much, do you?"

"I don't swim very well, but I like *this* boat."

"What makes this boat different?"

Without even seeming to think, she looked straight up in his eyes. "You're in this boat."

And that was all it took. "I'm sorry, Meg," Etienne said, "but I just have to kiss you now." And bracing his hands on the sides of the boat, bracketing her body with his hands, Etienne leaned forward and laid his lips on Meg's.

She was sweet, ripe, and twisting to meet him, totally

involved in the kiss, so much so that Etienne's heart began to pound, his hands began to sweat, his body ached with the need to do more.

But they were in a small boat and she didn't swim well.

He would die before he would let her fall out, but there was just no denying that this wasn't a very good place to kiss a woman.

Which was a good thing, his head told him. But his body told him something different.

Slowly he leaned back. He smiled at her. "Meg?"

"Yes?" Her voice was low and soft, her eyes were languorous.

"That was a wonderful distraction. Let's do it again. Somewhere else next time."

His comment had been meant to break the tension and make Meg laugh. Only no one was laughing.

And now all he was thinking about was how many more hours he had with her. And how he would manage to keep his mind off of her when she went home.

It had been a mistake, after all, to touch her again. Now he wanted her even more, but touching her… An honorable man didn't love a woman like Meg and then send her away. If he couldn't keep her—and he couldn't—he shouldn't even consider touching her.

But all he could think about when he looked at Meg was how much he wanted to hold her in his arms.

The time was slipping away and she was letting it happen, Meg thought the next morning. Ever since Etienne had kissed her and made that comment in the boat, the minutes and the march toward goodbye had seemed to fly faster and faster.

He'd shown her the rest of Mont Gavard, they'd

dined beneath the stars at Le Pre Catelan. Now there was just one last day before the expo and her return home.

"I want this to be memorable for you," Etienne said when he picked her up outside her door at the hotel where the expo would be held.

Meg laughed. "Etienne, it's Paris. It's memorable just by definition. It's the trip of a lifetime."

"All right, then, let's fit a lifetime into one day," he said.

They tried. They strolled along the Seine and the Champs-Elysées. They visited Sainte-Chapelle, Montmartre, the Arc de Triomphe and the Jardin des Tuileries.

Meg was usually the one who talked a mile a minute, but today it was Etienne, trying to fit as much into her day as possible. But the day was coming to a close. Standing by the water next to the pyramid at the Louvre, the sun began to sink as it always did. The sky put on a master performance and decked itself out in silver and red and gold and purple. There was a family nearby, a father playing with his two children, the mother looking on. The whole scene of Paris, the sunset, this gorgeous setting, the family was just…beautiful. Meg looked at the family lost in their own world and their own happiness and her throat closed up. She thought, that could be us.

But it couldn't be.

She looked up into Etienne's eyes. "Thank you. For showing me all this and for Mont Gavard," she said.

"I wish there had been more time. It wasn't enough."

She raised her hand and allowed herself the pleasure of touching his cheek. She ran her palm over his jaw. "It was more than I ever expected. I wasn't on the path to Paris when I met you."

He slowly pulled her close and gathered her in his

arms. He kissed her hair. "Don't try to make it sound as if I'm the one who made this happen. I've never brought anyone else to Paris."

She pulled back and looked at him. "Why not?"

"Because you're special. Don't make me say it again."

She didn't. Instead she rose on her toes and kissed him on the nose. He tilted his head and returned the kiss…on the lips, on that little scarred spot. Etienne groaned and kissed her there again, then dipped his head and kissed her throat.

Meg nearly fainted with pleasure.

A child coughed. Meg froze. "There are children nearby," she whispered.

Immediately Etienne released her. He took her hand. "I'll take you back," he said.

But when they made it to her hotel room door and she had the door open, Meg turned and faced Etienne. "There are *no* children nearby now," she said.

He laughed. He covered her mouth with his and tasted her. His hands went to her waist and climbed higher.

Heat flashed through Meg's body. She plunged her hands into his hair and gave kiss for kiss. "Come inside."

Etienne stopped kissing her. "Meg," he said. "I want you, but I don't want to be like Alan. I don't want to use you." His eyes were sad. He was like a piece of granite, unmoving when she tugged.

She stopped. Doubts assailed her. She had thought—

"You don't want me?"

Etienne's eyes opened wide, a shocked expression deepening their silver-blue. "I'm afraid of hurting you, but I'm not completely insane, Meg. I want you so much that it's killing me to stand here."

Meg stopped tugging. "You could never be like Alan,

Etienne. Alan wouldn't have cared about hurting me. But you're right. I don't want to hurt you, either. I don't want to force you. I don't want this to end on an unhappy note or ask you to do something you'll regret later. I don't want you to feel obligated to entertain me beyond the normal sightseeing or think that I expect kisses or more or—"

But she had barely got the last word out when Etienne scooped her up, carried her inside, kicked the door shut and dropped her on the bed. He came down on top of her, his arms braced so that his body wasn't touching hers. Much.

"Are you trying to manipulate me, Meg?"

She looked up into those glittering, gorgeous eyes, but she wasn't even vaguely afraid. Etienne might be frustrated but he would never intentionally hurt her. Still, she had goaded him into this and as much as she wanted him…

"I… Yes," she answered. "That is…not exactly, but…yes. Maybe. I don't really know. I wasn't even thinking straight. I just…want you, but I don't want to use you, either. I want our last days together to be happy. I want you to make love to me, but I also want you willingly, and if that can't happen and you're only here on this bed with me because I manipulated you here, then I would like a do-over, please. I would like to change my mind."

She couldn't keep the sad, sorry note out of her voice, and she absolutely hated that. What a pathetic woman. She tried to sit up.

Etienne didn't budge. "Meg, this suggestion of yours for a do-over intrigues me. Does that mean you no longer want *me*, *mon petit lapin*?" he whispered, dipping his head to nuzzle her neck.

Flames shot through Meg's body. When Etienne stopped his nuzzling and looked into her eyes again, some part of her that had survived the inferno managed to register that he was waiting for an answer. "I don't know what *mon petit lapin* means," she whispered.

He smiled and kissed her nose. "It's an affectionate term that roughly translates to my little rabbit."

She smiled slowly. "Affectionate?"

"Of course. Would I curse a woman who makes me as crazy to touch her as you do?"

"One wouldn't think so, Etienne, but…my little rabbit? That doesn't sound very sexy at all." She reached up and began to unbutton his shirt. Slowly.

Etienne took a deep, visible breath, his nostrils flaring slightly. "The term doesn't have to be sexy," he said, his voice raspy. "Because *you* are. Incredibly." He ran his palms down her body. She arched against him.

"I've been wanting to do this for a very long time, Etienne," she said, continuing to release his buttons. "I want us to end on the right note. I don't want you to have any regrets, and I don't want to have any regrets, either, so I'm getting you out of my system—completely—tonight. All right?"

He paused and gazed down into her eyes. "Promise me," he said. "Promise me that after I'm gone, you won't be sorry you let me touch you."

"I couldn't be sorry," she promised.

"Good. Because if you couldn't tell me that, I would have to stop, and…Meg…"

She placed her hands on his bare chest and whisked his shirt down his arms. "What, Etienne?" she whispered.

He shrugged out of his shirt and in only seconds had slid down the zipper that ran down the front of her dress, sliding the garment down and off her body. For long seconds he simply stared at her, his gaze moving slowly from her head down the length of her.

"Etienne?" Her voice came out on a choked gasp.

"That comment I made about stopping, Meg?"

"Yes?"

His eyes met hers. While he gazed at her he finished undressing her. "I'm not going to. Unless you ask me to. And I'm hoping that you won't ask."

"I'm asking you to make love with me, Etienne," she answered.

He smiled and shrugged out of his clothes, then took her in his arms. "You are the most amazing woman, Meg."

She pressed herself to him and took a deep, shuddering breath as his skin met hers. "And you are the most amazing man, Etienne. Please…amaze me."

But he did so much more than that. He kissed her, he caressed her.

She nipped at him and smoothed her palms over the chest she'd been wanting to touch.

He lifted her hair and made love to the nape of her neck. He made shivers run down her whole body, then followed with kisses that made her burn.

And then, he did something even more wonderful. He joined his body to hers. He turned her world to bliss. He made her forget everything but him.

Afterward, as they lay there half asleep, he held her and whispered in her ear, "Don't miss me when I'm gone, Meg," he said.

She kissed his hand. "Don't worry about me when I'm gone," she said.

But when morning came and he had returned to his room, Meg realized that neither of them had answered the other, and with good reason. She *was* going to miss him, and he *was* going to worry.

There was nothing she could do about the first. No matter what happened, she would miss him. How could she not when she loved him so much?

But as for the worrying about her, that couldn't be allowed to happen. Worrying that he had failed one woman, his wife, by walking away from her and leaving her on her own had nearly destroyed Etienne. That wasn't going to happen here. She was no fragile flower; she could take care of herself and she was darned sure going to show Etienne Gavard that he had absolutely nothing to worry about where Meg Leighton was concerned. She was totally capable of surviving completely on her own. He could leave her with a totally clean conscience.

He never needed to know that her heart was broken.

CHAPTER FIFTEEN

ETIENNE was worried. Ever since he and Meg had made love, she had been avoiding him. And when she hadn't been avoiding him, she'd been running full tilt. His concern wasn't because she looked unhappy. On the contrary, she was always smiling and cheerful. Extremely cheerful. More cheerful than any one person would ever be for that length of time. She even, occasionally, stopped and gave him one of those little pats on the cheek he had often seen her give her friends at Fieldman's. As if she was trying to reassure him. As if she was concerned for *him*. As if she was worried about *his* well-being.

When she knew very well that he had been the head of the Gavard family with all its lands, money, businesses and obligations for years. She knew things about his personal life, too. Above all, Meg knew that his Achilles' heel was vulnerable women.

All of which led him to believe that something wasn't right here. Because besides the fact that Meg was treating him as if he was merely a friend, she had not said one word about making love with him. Not a sound of regret, of joy, of anything. That just wasn't Meg. She was an emotional, involved, complex woman, and he was totally positive that she didn't take making love lightly.

Etienne fretted. He weighed the evidence…and decided that there could be only one likely conclusion. Meg was afraid that *he* would think she was falling in love with him and she was trying to protect him from beating up on himself.

That was exactly like Meg. And that really did make him worry. He didn't think she was falling in love with him. She'd made it clear from the beginning that long-term relationships with men held no appeal for her. She didn't even want to have a father hanging around when she finally had those babies she longed for. If he'd thought there was even a remote chance she might fall in love with him, he would… How *would* he feel?

For a minute his heart soared…and then fell. What did it matter how he felt? The truth was that he was all wrong for Meg. She wanted children; she needed a man who would stay in one place and be there for her. He was exactly the wrong kind of man for her. He was the kind who would end up hurting her even if he didn't want to. The fact that she was worrying about him was proof enough that her association with him was already taking its toll.

Especially since right now she had too much on her plate. She still had speeches to give at the expo, she had to fly home alone and then she had a company to run. From here on out, she would be shepherding her flock at Fieldman's alone. She didn't need to add "trying to make sure Etienne doesn't have any concerns" to her list of things to do.

What could he do? Tell her that she could stop

putting on an act for him? Tell her that he wasn't worried about her?

Well…he *was* worried about her, because…

Because I love her, he thought. The truth stared him in the face. He *loved* Meg. He would always worry about her, but those were the last things she needed to hear.

Her career was taking off. She was in demand. She was right where she had told him she wanted to be on that first day they met. A man like him…he'd merely been her springboard. Now he needed to get out of her way and let her do and be the things she wanted to do and be.

Etienne blew out a shaky breath. He resigned himself to letting Meg continue this charade. But he hated it. He didn't want her gentle pats on the cheek and her affectionate little smiles. What he wanted was all of her. Forever.

But he would *not* tell her that. It would just make her sad. And he would sacrifice anything if he could prevent Meg from suffering any more heartache in her life.

Meg never quite knew what happened on the last day of the expo. Everything had been going as planned. She had been meeting and greeting people, smiling, laughing, pasting on the "Face of Fieldman's" for the world to see. She had given some presentations. Orders had started pouring in, Jeff told her in a conference call.

But mostly she had been trying not to let Etienne know in any way that her heart was crumpling and cracking and that she was generally a mess inside whenever she thought about the fact that she would never see him again.

Still, she continued on. The hours were passing and she almost looked forward to the time when she could get on the plane and fly home, because then she could finally stop smiling and let herself cry.

She only had two more things to do before that could happen. First, she had to give one more presentation. And then, she had to kiss Etienne goodbye.

The second thing was the important one. No matter how much she had been avoiding him, she couldn't leave without being in his arms just once more. Just once. That would have to last her forever.

She was rushing to the presentation area and thinking about kissing Etienne, about where and when to do it and how long she could press her lips to his without him suspecting that she was totally in love with him, when she started to climb the five stairs to the makeshift stage, and the heel of her red stilettos clipped the last rung.

Most people would have been surprised by how quickly a person could go from standing upright at the top of a set of stairs to hitting the ground beneath, but Meg had taken all those classes she'd told Etienne about. In an attempt to garner some small measure of grace, she had been taught how to fall time and time again and had experienced the "upright to ground" phenomenon many times before, but in the past she had been concentrating so hard on trying to master the fall that she had inevitably failed.

Now, however, her first thought was that Etienne would witness her mishap and be either scared out of his wits or concerned that she still couldn't manage a simple walk across a room. In fact, she was sure she heard him cry out her name as she went down.

Consequently, somehow, Meg managed to gracefully roll and rise to her feet, brushing off her clothing and trying to simultaneously smile, rearrange her hair, pick up the papers she'd dropped, ignore the pain shooting through her body in various places and still be ready to turn and face Etienne as if nothing untoward had happened.

Too late. She was still disheveled, still missing papers when he vaulted over a table in his path and ran up beside her.

"Meg, *ma belle*, are you all right? What am I saying? Of course, you're not all right. You fell down the stairs. You must be damaged, Meg," he said in a rush as he reached for a chair, drew her to it and demanded that she sit down. Right then.

"Meg, *mon petit lapin*, look at me. Is that a bruise on your jaw?" His fingers gently brushed.

Meg melted. She leaned forward…and saw a world of worry in his eyes.

Slowly, she shook her head. She found a small smile. She touched his face. "Etienne, don't worry. Really. I'm fine. I did it. I finally learned how to execute a fall and live to tell the tale." She even laughed a little.

He wasn't laughing. His eyes looked stricken, scared. "Meg, you were wonderful, but…my heart may never be the same again. I was too far away, you were falling too fast. I was afraid you were going to hit your head, break something, worse. Meg, Meg…"

She couldn't help it. She framed his face with her hands and kissed him. "Etienne, I—"

"I can't leave you," he said suddenly. "It's too… You're too… Meg, I want you to marry me. Now."

Meg wasn't sure which one of them was more surprised to hear the words falling from his mouth. Etienne's gaze was fierce and intense and slightly shocked as if he wondered who had spoken, and Meg… For two seconds her heart overflowed with love and joy and…

No. She was totally sure that this proposal had been

an impetuous decision on his part, wrenched from him
by his concern for her. He'd been teaching her and
working with her for weeks and he was naturally concerned for her welfare, worried that he would fail her in
some way the way all teachers did. Then he'd seen her
fall and he had thought of Louisa, of how he'd failed his
wife. In some small way, not being able to be at Meg's
side when she'd fallen was reliving his past. This time
they'd shared had made him feel responsible for her, and
his suggestion that they marry was simply an attempt to
protect her and save her from future harm.

It was as she'd already admitted to herself. Etienne
saved people. But who saved Etienne from himself?

She would.

Meg slowly shook her head, she cupped his jaw, she
bent and kissed him. "Thank you, but I can't marry
you," she whispered. "It would be…so wrong."

Then she got up and stumbled out of the expo. She
didn't give her presentation. She didn't stop to sign out.
She just left.

The flight home was a blur. She vaguely remembered calling Edie and blurting out…something. She
sort of recalled Edie meeting her at the airport and how
she had sobbed in her tiny friend's arms.

After that, nothing much mattered or made sense or
sank in. There was a lot of sleeping, a lot of tears, a few
attempts to work and then more tears. She mindlessly
watched television. She sat for hours staring at nothing.

And then one day a few days later, the phone rang.

Meg stared at it, but didn't answer. Two minutes
later it rang again, and she picked it up, meaning to
hang up again.

Edie's panicked voice rang out. "Don't hang up,

Meg. Come quick. Alan is back, and he's threatening everyone in the office. He's making Paula cry."

Meg snapped to attention. "I'm on my way," was all she said before she hung up the phone and started to scramble for clothing.

Her heart was still raw, but that couldn't matter. She had neglected her friends and colleagues and there was no Etienne to save them. She had to put to use all that he'd taught her. She had to be the one.

The last time she and Alan had had a confrontation she had pushed back, but she'd had no real ammunition. Now she did. Etienne had given her what she needed.

Her heart lifted at the thought, and for the first time in a week she managed to smile.

Etienne probably broke every speeding law in the book on his way to Fieldman's after receiving Jeff's call. That jerk was terrorizing the employees and Jeff said that Edie had apparently gotten through to Meg after not being able to for most of the week.

Etienne thanked the stars above that he had returned to Chicago to begin the process of setting up the sale of the company to the employees. He only hoped he could reach Fieldman's before Meg did. *If that poor excuse for a man, Alan, does one thing to hurt her, I'll...*

You'll what? he asked himself. Already, he had made several wrong turns with Meg. That proposal... She'd been so proud of how she'd handled that fall and had he praised her? Well, maybe a little, but mostly he'd tried to corral her into marrying him. When he'd known that Meg had a strong need to be independent.

Nonetheless, he couldn't let Alan destroy her again. It was damned hard being a man in love, Etienne decided, as he slid into the parking lot at Fieldman's. Dammit. Meg's car was already here, parked crookedly across three spaces as if she'd arrived in a hurry.

Etienne's pulse began to thunder in his ears. She was in there with the man who had almost destroyed her. Swearing beneath his breath, Etienne started for the front door, then thought better of it and went around the back.

Everyone in the office was clustered up against the private offices as if they'd been herded there like cattle. Alan's voice rang out. "The contract has changed, because Gavard is selling it to you. That means you now have control, and I think you'll find that what I'm offering you is extremely generous. It could make a bundle for everyone here."

If steam could come out of a person's ears, it would be coming out of Etienne's now. He started to charge ahead, but then he saw Meg's face through the crowd. She was turned toward him and the man she faced had his back toward Etienne. The man was advancing and Etienne started to surge, but the expression on Meg's face wasn't one of fear. He saw determination and concentration and... Suddenly she lifted one eyebrow in a perfect expression of disbelief and condescension.

Etienne stopped moving forward. He noticed that Jeff and Edie had sidled up next to him. "Did you see that, my friend?" he whispered to Jeff. "What a wonderful woman!"

"Yeah, I was afraid that after she stayed holed up in her place all week that she was going to come out looking insane, but she's beautiful," Jeff whispered back.

A jolt went through Etienne. She was, indeed, beautiful, but...

"My Meg was locked up in her house?"

"Yes, what did you do to her?" Edie whispered. "I couldn't understand what she was telling me when she got off the plane, she was crying so hard."

Another jolt. "I proposed," he said.

"Oh. Did you say that you loved her?"

No, he hadn't. He shook his head.

Edie glared at him. "Well, that explains it, then," she replied. "If you didn't love her, you should never have proposed. Meg kept saying something about how you wanted to protect her and save her and she couldn't let you do that after what had happened to your wife and how you would always consider her a burden and a responsibility. The rest was hard to hear. She was pretty broken up."

Ah, he'd botched things badly. How had he done that to his lovely Meg? But he couldn't ask any more questions now. He was straining to listen to Meg. After her eyebrow-raising, Alan had gone off on some rambling attempt to make his case. Now, she was crossing her arms and stepping forward.

Alan took a step backward, closer to the rabble behind him. It was a bit like the French revolution revisited. Etienne wanted nothing more than to beat the man senseless for daring to even speak to Meg, but after Edie's comments, he saw where he had gone wrong. Meg needed to be strong, to earn her place in life. People had always forced her into a weak position. They'd made her feel that her strengths were weaknesses, but a man who loved her would never do that. He wouldn't insist on saving her. He'd let her fight…unless she asked for his help.

"I believe you were told that you weren't to approach anyone in this company," Meg was saying. "I think it's more than safe to say that you have stepped over the line, Alan."

"I believe that if this company is employee-owned, then you don't get to make all the decisions, Meg. This sounds like you're just upset because I scorned you and dumped you."

Etienne jumped forward a little before Edie and Jeff grabbed him and before he got control of himself. He swore…in French. Too loudly. Alan apparently was too worked up to hear, but Meg's head immediately came up. She looked straight into Etienne's eyes.

Then she smiled.

"I could see where you might think something like that, Alan, and I probably can't change your mind. You always did think a lot more of yourself than anyone else did. But the truth is that I've…um…been involved with men that are far better, more admirable, and ten times more handsome than you'll ever be, so no, the woman scorned thing just isn't doing it for me. Try something else."

"How about this?" Alan turned to the crowd. "I'll pay you a lot more than Meg will ever make for you."

A murmur went through the crowd. "Wow, is that true, Meg?" Paula asked.

"I don't know. Maybe," Meg said. "But do you really want to ever work for a jerk like this?"

"Hmm, no, but I *would* like to throw a bottle at his head," Paula said.

"Or worse," someone yelled. "He hurt Meg. We don't want to have anything to do with someone like that no matter how much money he offers. What can we do to make him leave?"

Meg looked up into Etienne's eyes. "I believe that

this might be a question for my advisor," she said, nodding to Etienne.

Jeff let go of Etienne's arm and he moved forward, making a beeline for Meg. "There are various possibilities here," Etienne offered. "He's been warned to stay away, so we might consider him a trespasser."

"Hah! That'll never stick," Alan said.

"I believe I was talking to Meg," Etienne said. "And yes, it probably wouldn't stick…yet," he told her. "But we could establish a precedent, file a complaint and eventually manage to bar him from the property. After that he could be arrested."

Meg nodded solemnly. "I like that idea. Not as much as the hitting him with the bottle, but it does have the appeal of being legal."

"Or we could have his car towed. Right now. It's an unauthorized vehicle in the parking lot, isn't it?"

A cry went up from the rabble. "Yeah, he's got a really expensive car. I'd love to see that on the back of a tow truck. Let's go call right now and we'll stand guard so he can't drive it away," someone said.

Alan swore.

"Alan, shame on you. Such language," Meg said. "I don't like swearing in the office…unless it's in French. Yes, let's definitely tow his car."

Alan swore again. And then he ran for the door.

A round of applause went up from the rabble standing behind Etienne. He walked forward and pulled Meg into his arms. "I know this is unprofessional, but I just have to do it," he said. "You were *magnifique, mon coeur*." When his lips met hers, Etienne's heart began to pound. She was all he wanted and needed, but he had to let her go.

CHAPTER SIXTEEN

Etienne turned to leave, and Meg's heart skipped. She held out her hand. "Thank you," she said. "But…" It was going to be so hard to ask this. It was opening a conversation that might end so badly, so awkwardly, so heartbreakingly. "You know I don't know much French. What did you call me just then?"

His smile was sad. "My heart. It's an affectionate term."

"Like my little rabbit?"

Now his eyes were sad, too. "A bit, but…more."

Her throat felt so full she could barely speak, but…he was going to leave. If he left…

"I never thanked you," she said. "So…thank you."

"For this? This was all you," he answered.

"For the proposal."

"Meg, I'm so sorry for that. It wasn't meant to be an insult."

"I know. You were worried about me. You wanted to protect me."

"And yet, today you didn't need protecting."

Her heart was aching, and yet she laughed. "It felt like I needed protecting at times. I was afraid and angry and not thinking all that clearly at first, but yes, I managed, because I remembered things you had told me. You gave me courage. You made me realize that I could be me, and that being Meg Leighton was a good thing."

"It's a wonderful thing."

"I wondered… You didn't even try to step in with Alan today. That's so…not like you."

A pale imitation of that wonderful grin appeared, and pale as it was, her heart still leaped. "I wanted to. For a few seconds, Jeff and Edie were holding on to me so that I couldn't rush forward, but mostly I held back because I realized that you didn't need my help. At all. You didn't need saving. Meg, I have to be honest… You have to know that I'll always want to save you and protect you. Always. Forever. I can't seem to help it. You do that to me, but I also want you to know that I wouldn't, unless you asked. That proposal…"

She tried to shrug and to look as if she didn't care. "It was an impulsive thing, I know. You felt you had to do it."

The pale grin was gone. Etienne's eyes burned fire. "Meg, look at me. I love you. It might have been out of the blue, but it wasn't remotely impulsive. It was because I couldn't do anything else. When a man feels about a woman the way I feel about you… I love you, Meg. You've turned my world around and I just can't help loving you."

A tear slipped off her lashes and fell.

"Meg, *mon coeur*, I've made you cry," he whispered in wonder. "You never cry."

"I know."

"Why? Have I hurt you?"

She shook her head vigorously. "Do you think... I'm sure I hurt your pride when I told you I couldn't marry you, but do you think... I mean... I do love you, Etienne. So very much. I hated telling you no when I wanted to say yes and..."

He pulled her into his arms right then and there. "While I was here, I bought a piece of property. At the time I didn't know what I would do with it, but now... I'm thinking of a second Mont Gavard. I'd build a house, maybe get a cat and... If I asked you to marry me, again, Meg, would I hurt you again?"

She turned in his arms. She pressed her lips to his. When she pulled away, she stared directly into his eyes. "I don't know if that was a hypothetical question, Etienne, but please ask me again. I know your work takes you far away, and much as I'll miss you when you're gone, I'm strong. I can handle your absences...or I'll travel with you. You don't have to build the house or get a cat or...anything but...just love me."

"I love you now. I'll love you forever. I'm asking you again. And I'll ask as many times as it takes. Marry me, Meg. Love me. And yes, we *are* building the house. You may be strong enough for the separations, but I couldn't be apart from you that long. We'll delegate, bring new people into the business. We'll make a family, Meg."

"And we'll travel back and forth between France and here?"

"Whatever you want, love. Wherever you are is home to me."

Meg smiled through her tears. "I'm so glad Alan dumped me and fired me. If he hadn't, you wouldn't be here."

Etienne laughed. "What an amazing way of thinking

you have, love. And yes, I agree with you. I'm grateful for anything that brought us to this moment, but don't expect me to send the man a thank you card. And Meg?"

She looked up and waited.

"The eyebrow thing?"

She blushed. "Lots of practice. I'm very good at practicing."

"You're very good at lots of things, and I intend to learn about every single one of them, my love, my heart, my everything, my Meg."

"Mon petit lapin," she whispered to him. *"Mon coeur."*

"Look at that. Meg's speaking French," someone whispered.

"And our bosses are kissing. This is the best place in the world to work." That was Paula's voice.

Etienne and Meg chuckled. He whispered in Meg's ear. She whispered back. Then she turned to the group.

"Etienne and I would like to declare this a paid holiday for all of you," she said. "Beginning right this minute."

A cheer went up.

"Best ever place to work!" someone else agreed. "Kiss her again, Etienne."

"Oh, I intend to," he said. "Many times. Kissing Meg will be the greatest joy in my life. It's going to be at the top of my to do list every day, at the bottom, and lots of places in between." He twirled Meg into his arms and against his heart. She was a perfect fit.

"Now, about that list," she said.

He smiled. "It's written on my heart, but this is how it begins." He kissed her.

"And this is how *my* list continues," she whispered, returning his kiss.

He smiled against her lips. "I like the way you think, my love. I always have."

"Show me," she said.

"*Toujours, always,*" he said. Then he kissed her again.

* * * * *

The helicopter swung abruptly sideways in a dizzying arch, setting Jack McCall's fever-ravaged brain spinning.

His friend's voice sounded tinny, coming through the earphones. "You belong in a hospital," he said. "Not some backwater bed-and-breakfast."

All Jack really knew about the virus raging through his system was that it wasn't contagious, and there was no known treatment for it besides a lot of rest and quiet. "I don't like hospitals," he responded, hoping he sounded like his normal self. "They're full of sick people."

Vince Griffin chuckled but it was a dry sound, rough at the edges. "What's in Stone Creek, Arizona?" he asked. "Besides a whole lot of nothin'?"

Ashley O'Ballivan was in Stone Creek, and she was a whole lot of somethin', but Jack had neither the strength nor the inclination to explain. After the way he'd ducked out six months before, he didn't expect a welcome, knew he didn't deserve one. But Ashley, being Ashley, would take him in whatever her misgivings.

He had to get to Ashley; he'd be all right.

He closed his eyes, letting the fever swallow him. There was no telling how much time had passed when he became aware of the chopper blades slowing overhead. Dimly, he saw the private ambulance waiting on the airfield outside of Stone Creek; it seemed that twilight had descended.

Jack sighed with relief. His clothes felt clammy against his flesh. His teeth began to chatter as two figures unloaded a gurney from the back of the ambulance and waited for the blades to stop.

"Great," Vince remarked, unsnapping his seat belt. "Those two look like volunteers, not real EMTs."

The chopper bounced sickeningly on its runners, and Vince, with a shake of his head, pushed open his door and jumped to the ground, head down.

Jack waited, wondering if he'd be able to stand on his own. After fumbling unsuccessfully with the buckle on his seat belt, he decided not.

When it was safe the EMTs approached, following Vince, who opened Jack's door.

His old friend Tanner Quinn stepped around Vince, his grin not quite reaching his eyes.

"You look like hell warmed over," he told Jack cheerfully.

"Since when are you an EMT?" Jack retorted.

Tanner reached in, wedged a shoulder under Jack's right arm and hauled him out of the chopper. His knees immediately buckled, and Vince stepped up, supporting him on the other side.

"In a place like Stone Creek," Tanner replied, "everybody helps out."

They reached the wheeled gurney, and Jack found himself on his back.

Tanner and the second man strapped him down, a process that brought back a few bad memories.

"Is there even a hospital in this place?" Vince asked irritably from somewhere in the night.

"There's a pretty good clinic over in Indian Rock," Tanner answered easily, "and it isn't far to Flagstaff." He paused to help his buddy hoist Jack and the gurney into the back of the ambulance. "You're in good hands, Jack. My wife is the best veterinarian in the state."

Jack laughed raggedly at that.

Vince muttered a curse.

Tanner climbed into the back beside him, perched on some kind of fold-down seat. The other man shut the doors.

"You in any pain?" Tanner said as his partner climbed into the driver's seat and started the engine.

"No." Jack looked up at his oldest and closest friend and wished he'd listened to Vince. Ever since he'd come down with the virus—a week after snatching a five-year-old girl back from her non-custodial parent, a small-time Colombian drug dealer—he hadn't been able to think about anyone or anything but Ashley. When he *could* think, anyway.

Now, in one of the first clearheaded moments he'd experienced since checking himself out of Bethesda the day before, he realized he might be making a major mistake. Not by facing Ashley—he owed her that much and a lot more. No, he could be putting her in danger, putting Tanner and his daughter and his pregnant wife in danger, too.

"I shouldn't have come here," he said, keeping his voice low.

Tanner shook his head, his jaw clamped down hard as though he was irritated by Jack's statement.

"This is where you belong," Tanner insisted. "If

you'd had sense enough to know that six months ago, old buddy, when you bailed on Ashley without so much as a fare-thee-well, you wouldn't be in this mess."

Ashley. The name had run through his mind a million times in those six months, but hearing somebody say it out loud was like having a fist close around his insides and squeeze hard.

Jack couldn't speak.

Tanner didn't press for further conversation.

The ambulance bumped over country roads, finally hitting smooth blacktop.

"Here we are," Tanner said. "Ashley's place."

* * * * *

Will Jack be able to patch things up with Ashley,
or will his past put the woman he loves
in harm's way?
Find out in
AT HOME IN STONE CREEK
by Linda Lael Miller
Available November 2009
from Silhouette Special Edition®

This November,
Silhouette Special Edition®
brings you

NEW·YORK TIMES
BESTSELLING AUTHOR

LINDA LAEL
MILLER

At Home in
Stone Creek

Available in November
wherever books are sold.

HARLEQUIN *Romance*.

This November,
queen of the rugged rancher

PATRICIA THAYER

teams up with

DONNA ALWARD

*to bring you an extra-special treat
this holiday season—*

two romantic stories
in one book!

Join sisters Amelia and Kelley for Christmas at
Rocking H Ranch where these feisty cowgirls swap
presents for proposals, mistletoe for marriage and
experience the unbeatable rush of falling in love!

Available in November wherever books are sold.

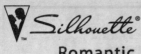

Romantic
SUSPENSE

**Sparked by Danger,
Fueled by Passion.**

*Blackout
At Christmas*

Beth Cornelison,
Sharron McClellan,
Jennifer Morey

What happens when a major blackout shuts
down the entire Western seaboard on Christmas
Eve? Follow stories of danger, intrigue and
romance as three women learn to trust their
instincts to survive and open their hearts to the
love that unexpectedly comes their way.

*Available November
wherever books are sold.*

Visit Silhouette Books at www.eHarlequin.com

SRS27653

REQUEST YOUR FREE BOOKS!
2 FREE NOVELS PLUS 2
FREE GIFTS!

HARLEQUIN®

Romance®

From the Heart, For the Heart

YES! Please send me 2 FREE Harlequin® Romance novels and my 2 FREE gifts (gifts are worth about $10). After receiving them, if I don't wish to receive any more books, I can return the shipping statement marked "cancel". If I don't cancel, I will receive 4 brand-new novels every month and be billed just $3.84 per book in the U.S. or $4.24 per book in Canada. That's a savings of at least 15% off the cover price! It's quite a bargain! Shipping and handling is just 50¢ per book.* I understand that accepting the 2 free books and gifts places me under no obligation to buy anything. I can always return a shipment and cancel at any time. Even if I never buy another book, the two free books and gifts are mine to keep forever.

114 HDN EYU3 314 HDN EYKG

Name _____ (PLEASE PRINT)

Address _____ Apt. #

City _____ State/Prov. _____ Zip/Postal Code

Signature (if under 18, a parent or guardian must sign)

Mail to the **Harlequin Reader Service:**
IN U.S.A.: P.O. Box 1867, Buffalo, NY 14240-1867
IN CANADA: P.O. Box 609, Fort Erie, Ontario L2A 5X3

Not valid to current subscribers of Harlequin Romance books.

**Are you a subscriber of Harlequin Romance books
and want to receive the larger-print edition?
Call 1-800-873-8635 today!**

* Terms and prices subject to change without notice. Prices do not include applicable taxes. Sales tax applicable in N.Y. Canadian residents will be charged applicable provincial taxes and GST. Offer not valid in Quebec. This offer is limited to one order per household. All orders subject to approval. Credit or debit balances in a customer's account(s) may be offset by any other outstanding balance owed by or to the customer. Please allow 4 to 6 weeks for delivery. Offer available while quantities last.

Your Privacy: Harlequin Books is committed to protecting your privacy. Our Privacy Policy is available online at www.eHarlequin.com or upon request from the Reader Service. From time to time we make our lists of customers available to reputable third parties who may have a product or service of interest to you. If you would prefer we not share your name and address, please check here. ☐

HR09R

HARLEQUIN
Ambassadors

Want to share your passion for reading Harlequin® Books?

Become a Harlequin Ambassador!

Harlequin Ambassadors are a group of passionate and well-connected readers who are willing to share their joy of reading Harlequin® books with family and friends.

You'll be sent all the tools you need to spark great conversation, including free books!

All we ask is that you share the romance with your friends and family!

You'll also be invited to have a say in new book ideas and exchange opinions with women just like you!

To see if you qualify* to be a Harlequin Ambassador, please visit www.HarlequinAmbassadors.com.

*Please note that not everyone who applies to be a Harlequin Ambassador will qualify. For more information please visit www.HarlequinAmbassadors.com.

Thank you for your participation.

BAP09BPA

Coming Next Month

Available November 10, 2009

For an early surprise this Christmas don't look under the
Christmas tree or in your stocking—look out for
Christmas Treats in your November Harlequin® Romance novels!

#4129 MONTANA, MISTLETOE, MARRIAGE
Christmas Treats
Patricia Thayer and Donna Alward
Join sisters Amelia and Kelley for Christmas on Rocking H Ranch as we
bring you two stories in one volume for double the romance!

#4130 THE MAGIC OF A FAMILY CHRISTMAS Susan Meier
Christmas Treats
All six-year-old Harry wants for Christmas is for his new mom, Wendy, to
marry so they can be a forever family. Will his wish come true?

#4131 CROWNED: THE PALACE NANNY Marion Lennox
Marrying His Majesty
When powerful prince Stefanos meets feisty nanny Elsa, sparks fly!
But will she ever agree to *Marrying His Majesty*? Find out in the final
installment of this majestic trilogy.

#4132 CHRISTMAS ANGEL FOR THE BILLIONAIRE Liz Fielding
Trading Places
Lady Rosanne Napier is *Trading Places* with a celebrity look-alike to
escape the spotlight and meets the man of her dreams in the start of
this brand-new duet.

#4133 COWBOY DADDY, JINGLE-BELL BABY Linda Goodnight
Christmas Treats
On a dusty Texas roadside, cowboy Dax delivers Jenna's baby. When he
offers her a job, neither expects her to become his housekeeper bride!

#4134 UNDER THE BOSS'S MISTLETOE Jessica Hart
Christmas Treats
Cassie was determined to ignore the attraction she felt for her new boss,
but that was before she was forced to pose under the mistletoe with
delectable Jake!